ONE DAY
ON THE
RIVER RED

ALSO BY TIMOTHY J. KLOBERDANZ

Once Upon the River Platte (forthcoming)

*Sundogs and Sunflowers: Folklore and Folk Art of the
Northern Great Plains* (co-editor)

We Remember: Stories of the Germans from Russia
(co-editor)

*Thunder on the Steppe: Volga German Folklife in a
Changing Russia* (co-author)

Readings in Introductory Anthropology (co-editor)

Plains Folk: North Dakota's Ethnic History
(co-author)

*The Volga Germans in Old Russia and in Western
North America: Their Changing Worldview*

As High as the Eagle Flies

The Tragedy at Summit Springs

ONE DAY ON THE RIVER RED

a novella by

Timothy J. Kloberdanz

★ Legendary Rivers of the American West Series ★

CLOVIS HOUSE
Fargo, North Dakota

Clovis House
P.O. Box 1957
Fargo, North Dakota 58107-1957
www.clovishouse.com

Cover photo: "Sky Fall on the Red River" © Dave Bruner
Author photo: © Clovis House
Book design: Jenay

ISBN 978-0-9993712-2-0 (paperback)
ISBN 978-0-9993712-3-7 (e-book)
LCCN 2018910572

A portion of the profits from the sale of this book will be donated to the St. Jude Children's Research Hospital®

FIRST EDITION

PRINTED IN THE UNITED STATES OF AMERICA

In memory of

Margaret (Kloberdanz) Sewald

As a youngster, she worked in countless fields
along the Red River of the North. Sometimes,
at the end of a long day of thinning and hoeing
sugar beets, she and her brothers and sisters
would play at the river's edge. In later years,
Margaret married, had two daughters, and died
at the age of twenty-six.

Shadows
    they creep ahead
    enshrouding the woods
    of the trickster river red.

Shadows
    so much unsaid
    these restless souls
    of the living and the dead.

"I still haven't figured out this thing called 'life.' Not sure if I ever will. You see, life is just too big and too complicated. A little ant can take on a great big watermelon, but that little ant can't take on the whole world. There are limits, you know. . . ."

—Raymond O. Knutson

Contents

PROLOGUE

An Old Legend

Once, a long time ago, an artisan had a blacksmith shop on a high riverbank. It was an ideal location because two different rivers came together at that spot. When they merged, the two rivers formed a third and much larger river. People later would refer to that third river as *la Riviére Rouge du Nord*—the Red River of the North.

The artisan was very old, so he slept most of the time. He used his large stone anvil for a bed. The artisan only worked when there was a long lightning storm, the kind without any thunder. Even in the middle of the night, a nonstop lightning storm could light up the sky for hours and hours.

During one such storm, the old artisan forged a golden ring with three interwoven strands. Each of the three strands represented the three rivers in that locality.

The artisan knew the golden ring was very special and very powerful. So he threw it into the waters of the Red River of the North for safekeeping. Then the old artisan stretched out on the large stone anvil. He was very tired. And he went to sleep for a long, long time.

RAYMOND'S STORY

CHAPTER 1

*T*erminal. If you hear that word at an airport, it's okay. You expect to hear it. But when a doctor in a white coat sits across from you and tells you that your condition is terminal, well, that's a whole different story. Like the younger folks are so fond of saying these days, it sucks. It really sucks.

Terminal. What a word. It doesn't allow a person much hope, does it? Yet people crave hope. We hope for a good life. We hope for a better future. Even when things are at their worst, we somehow hope for the best.

Terminal. That one word threatens to dash all hope. A word like that snuffs out dreams. And that one word mocks everything that is dear and precious about life itself.

Terminal. The more I say that word, the madder I get. But I just noticed something. Every time I say or even think the word, I seem to lessen its effect a bit. So maybe I need to give all this a different spin.

Maybe there's a bright side, a silver lining even to the dark cloud of utter hopelessness. And maybe, just maybe, I can figure out a way to take control of things and beat death at its own cruel little game. Besides, why dread the inevitable?

"If you gotta kiss an ugly toad, just do it!" That's what Grandma Alma Knutson would say when we kids procrastinated and didn't want to do something unpleasant—like cleaning the outhouse or castrating calves or throwing up chili dogs. "Don't put it off. Just get it over with," she'd tell us.

Well, what would Grandma Knutson say if she saw me now, standing on the edge of the Red River? (The river isn't really red, by the way. It's more of a light brown color.) Grandma often referred to this river as the "River Red." When anyone dared to correct her, Grandma would remind them that she and Grandpa saw a famous movie in the 1950s called *The Bridge on the River Kwai*. After that, Grandma insisted on saying the "River Red." She said referring to a river that way sounded more dignified and respectful.

Oh, but if Grandma Knutson saw me now, she would wonder why I'm practically standing in the "River Red" and putting all these big, dirty rocks in my pockets. One of the bigger rocks is nice and clean. It's one that I brought from the front of my house. I kept an extra house key under that rock for many years. Early this morning, I washed off the rock and dried it real good. And then, on the smoothest side of the rock, I wrote:

ROK
RAYMOND O. KNUTSON
No inquiry needed.
I did this my way.

That's what the rock says. I do hope this rock will do its job. It's supposed to identify my soggy remains after I've been in the water for a long time. More than that, the rock will help do me in and free me all at the same time. So this is an important rock. I guess you could say it's a multipurpose rock.

I wrote the words on the rock with a black felt pen—a pen that was labeled "permanent." We'll see just how permanent the words will be once this rock is under the brown waters of the Red River for a few days (or weeks or months). Maybe no one will miss me. Perhaps I should have used some kind of heavy duty, water-resistant, black enamel paint like the kind I sold in my hardware store for so many years? I used to care about stuff like that. I really cared. But today I just want to get this over with.

You see, it's fall now. And this has been a rather damp and dreary October. Everything is dying—the flowers, the plants, even the grass. Dead leaves cover the ground and some of the trees look like skeletons. At times like this, when so many leaves are falling, it feels like the whole sky is falling.

Last Thursday was the day I got the news that I am "terminal." So why go through all of those long cold months of winter that lie ahead? According to the wooly caterpillars I've seen, it's going to be quite a winter. A real "doozy," as the old-timers say.

I look down at my hands. They are covered with age spots and freckles. There was this Irish fellow who came into my store one time. When he saw my freckled hands, he told me I must have "Celtic" ties of some kind. Celtic? I explained that, freckles or no freckles, I was pure Norwegian. But the guy didn't give an inch. He claimed the Vikings used to raid Ireland, and so a lot of real pure people got real mixed up.

As that Irish fellow left my store, he told me I should be proud of my "Irish" ancestors because they gave America things like Halloween. Yeah, right. Well, I won't be seeing another Halloween this year. Doubt if I'll miss it. I certainly won't have to dish out handfuls of candy or shovel off any pieces of smashed pumpkins from my driveway.

At four o'clock this morning, when I woke up, I didn't have much of an appetite. Half an hour later, I did get a little hungry. All I wanted was just one banana. But all four of the bananas that I had in the kitchen had turned black and were getting kinda soft. Instead of throwing them away, I left the black bananas on the kitchen table, next to a long envelope on which I had written "TO WHOM IT MAY CONCERN." Yeah, today is not just a bad day. It's a "black bananas bad day."

When I still owned the hardware store, I had a small office in back where I did most of my paperwork. There was a hand-lettered sign over the desk that had been there since I bought the place. It said: "Today is the day spawned by yesterday's tomorrow." When I looked at that sign and really thought about it for a while, it kinda gave me a headache. But I never took the sign down. The truth is, I left it there for the next owner to ponder.

Well, today is yesterday's tomorrow. And today is *the day*. I want to reach down and pick up just one more big rock, but I am so weighted down I can hardly touch my knees. My pants pockets and coat pockets are crammed full. I once read somewhere that when people enter the water and do what I am about to do, they sometimes change their minds. But I don't want to be one of those wishy-washy types. Oh, no. When I set out to do something, I follow through. Come hell or high water. Wow. Suddenly, I have all these water images and phrases in my head. Staring into a river does that, you know.

Uff da! That is what we Norwegians say when we get exasperated. When we really get excited (which isn't too often), we take it up a notch or two and we say *"Uff da fida!"*

Look at me. I can hardly walk. Like an overstuffed duck, I have to waddle into the river. And this water is ice cold! Well, if I don't sink and drown, I will catch my death of cold. Yeah, my death of cold. The river is so incredibly cold that I can feel my temperature actually dropping every second.

What prayer should I say? I cannot think of the right one. Is there a special prayer for those about to commit the ultimate act of self-destruction? Imagine what my Lutheran minister would say if I asked him about that. But I do need some kind of prayer. Not sure why, but the Lord's Prayer doesn't seem quite right. And the prayer before meals certainly doesn't fit. Funny, but all I can think of is a Catholic prayer that I often heard my late wife Tillie say. I'm not sure what it was called, but in it were the words "pray for us sinners now and at the hour of our death." Those Catholics, they don't beat around the bush. And they don't sugar-coat anything. Well, here I am, the new rock collector and aging sinner Raymond Knutson, sinking into the ice-cold waters of the great Red River of the North. And it is happening "now" and this is "the hour" of my death. Talk about heavy!

The side current of the river is trying to push me downstream, but I am so weighted down that I could not make it back to shore even if I wanted to. Well, I think this is it. I keep moving, but I am taking baby steps. And ever so slowly, I am getting into the main current. Soon this dirty brown water will be up to my neck and all over my face. So why did I wash up early this morning, when I'm going to wash up on shore anyway?

For some reason, I hear Grandma Knutson again. She has been gone for many years, but I keep hearing her Norwegian sing-song voice this morning. Whenever we were in a car and going over the "River Red" or any river, Grandma Knutson reminded us to touch the roof of the car and say:

> *Nix, nix, nix!*
> *Calm the rivers,*
> *Calm the cricks.*
> *No more troubles,*
> *No more tricks.*
> *Nix, nix, nix!*

I now say the words, mimicking Grandma Knutson and her Norwegian accent. But I have to do this right. Instead of touching the roof of a car, I try to raise my right hand to touch the roof of the sky. It will be kind of a goodbye gesture. But it is of no use. I

21

can barely move my limbs. Now I am in midstream and I feel the river take hold of me. It is really showing me its power. Ice-cold water rushes into my mouth and nostrils. My God, I am being water-boarded by a river!

Yes, I know. I asked for all of this. And I want to accept my fate like the seventy-year-old senior citizen and long-time member of the Sons of Norway that I am. We Scandinavians are supposed to be strong and stoic. But this is anything but easy. I am thinking that sleeping pills and lying under some nice warm blankets, all that would have been a lot easier. And certainly cleaner and more comfortable. Death be not proud, you know.

I am completely submerged under the freezing waters. These rocks are doing their job. But I am kinda disappointed, because I don't see any bright light at the end of the tunnel or any dead relatives coming to greet me. Not yet, anyway. It's almost impossible to see anything down here.

Suddenly, I feel something taking off my shoes and tugging at my pants. My belt is being loosened and my pants are being pulled down to my ankles. *Uff da!*

First, I am water-boarded by a river and now I am being stripped and violated by the same river. I am definitely having second thoughts. This death thing isn't at all what I expected.

Oh my! There go my pants. They're completely off now. *Uff da fida!*

CHAPTER 2

Startling green eyes. I don't know how else to describe them. They are startling green and they are only inches away. And they are looking into my own pale blue, watery eyes. Strange, but I do not remember any dead relatives who had such piercing green eyes.

I am on my back and I am wet and shivering. A young woman with long red hair and startling green eyes kneels over me. She continues to stare into my eyes, as if she is checking to see if I am really alive.

"Are you alright?" she asks.

But I cannot answer. I am shaking so bad that I can't utter a word. And I am trying to remember all that has just happened.

The young woman moves over my body and covers it with her own. At times, I can feel her warm breath on my face and neck. Then she slowly rises up and vigorously rubs my upper body with hands that are incredibly soft and warm. Soon she massages my legs and feet.

"I had to pull off your pants and shoes because they were weighing you down. What were you doing in the river?"

I do not want to say. And I'm unable to speak anyway. I simply motion toward a big gray house on the hill behind us.

"Is that where you live? Maybe if I help you up and then get you inside, you'll be able to warm up. If I help you, do you think you can make it up the hill to your house? Do you think you can do that?"

This is a lot to process and I am not myself. I nod, but I am still shaking. Suddenly, I am feeling terribly embarrassed that I am in my underwear. As the woman helps me stand up, water pours out of my briefs. I am not urinating, but it sure sounds like it. And there are at least three streams. She probably thinks I'm deformed or something.

I realize that I have to get out of these clothes (few as they are) and get inside my house as quickly as possible. The neighborhood I live in is a small one, and Mrs. Gunderson (two houses down) and some of the other folks do love to look out their windows and to talk. Usually, they talk about nothing. But this, this is something.

As I start to walk, one of the big stones rolls out of my coat pocket. It makes a squishy thud as it drops.

"What's with all of the rocks?" the green-eyed woman asks. But she seems to know why and she takes out each of the wet rocks, one by one. She is surprised by how many there are. When she gets to the last one, she sees what I had written on the biggest of the stones.

"ROK?—I think you misspelled 'ROCK'," she says. "Are you Raymondo Knutson?"

Raymondo? Do I look like a Raymondo? I don't have the energy to correct her and explain everything. But I do try to retrieve the telltale rock. It was a good one for concealing the house key. She hurls the weighty stone into the river. I am too slow. There is a loud splash and then everything is quiet again. Funny, but suddenly I feel like I have lost an old friend.

"You don't need it, Raymondo. Let the river have it."

The green-eyed woman is also sopping wet. As we both walk

uphill, we leave a double trail of dripping water and muddy footprints. I am still unsteady on my feet, but the woman has her arm tight around my waist and she guides and supports me. Her body feels incredibly strong and even warm, despite her wet clothing. She wears an old-fashioned blouse and pants that do not match. Her socks and slippers also are unusual. Oh, the dress styles of the younger folks these days! I cannot keep up.

When we reach my front door, it is just my luck that Mrs. Gunderson (who pretends to dust off her mailbox) sees me standing in my wet underwear. And here I am, next to a much younger and thoroughly drenched woman. Mrs. Gunderson does quite a doubletake. All I can do is give her one of those glances that says "well, it's a long story."

For a couple of minutes, I search for the outside house key. Finally, I remember that I used the rock that once concealed it for my last words. Now that rock is long gone. But on leaving the house this morning, I decided to place the key under the front doormat, where the police could easily find it. I reach down and the young woman helps me as we lift up the doormat and uncover the key.

Her hands are warm and steady as they guide my own.

"You need to come inside and dry off, too," I finally am able to say.

She looks around as if she is a bit uncertain.

"You don't have to invite me in," she whispers. "I'll be fine."

"Nonsense," I answer. "We both need to warm up. We've had quite a morning."

As the front door opens, I turn to the young woman.

"Forgive my poor manners. I haven't even asked your name."

The young woman stares at me with those startling green eyes, and she lightly touches my shoulder to make the introduction even more memorable.

"I'm Jewel."

CHAPTER 3

While Jewel showers upstairs, I clean up in the basement bathroom. Since the laundry room is close by, I throw Jewel's clothes into the washer. Poor girl, her clothes seem so old and worn.

Before Jewel went into the shower, I gave her some of Tillie's clothes to wear, including some red socks. What can I say? Tillie loved wearing red socks and red shoes. They were her trademark, you know.

Jewel is in the shower quite a long time. That gives me a chance to put away the "TO WHOM IT MAY CONCERN" envelope that was on the kitchen table. I brew some coffee and I fill the kitchen table with boxes of cereal, milk, bread, butter, jam, cookies, wieners, and all the other breakfast food that I can find.

When Jewel enters the kitchen, I am taken aback. Physically, she looks nothing like my Tillie. But the sight of Jewel in my dead wife's clothes, well, it kinda gets to me. Jewel even wears the long red socks, and the color brings out the redness of her long and freshly-combed hair. Now, standing in my kitchen, Jewel looks smaller and almost frail to me. How, I wonder, did this young woman manage to pull me out of the river? She must lift weights or something.

I motion for Jewel to sit down at the kitchen table and she seems uncertain what to do next. I pour her a cup of coffee and fill it to the brim. When she takes the first sip, she winces. After I put a fair amount of sugar and cream into her coffee, she seems more appreciative of its taste.

In the middle of the table is a tall carton of whole milk. Jewel reads aloud the words on the carton as if she is deciphering a long-lost and complex code from another civilization: "Grade A. Homogenized. Pasteurized."

"Those are just buzzwords to assure customers that the milk is safe and of high quality," I tell Jewel. "And it's probably free from any artificial growth hormones. One can't be too careful these days."

"Could I try some of those?" Jewel asks, pointing to the black bananas that I had forgotten to throw into the waste basket.

"Oh no, Jewel, you don't want those. They're overripe and they've gone soft."

"I like soft food," she declares. "And besides, food should never go to waste."

Shaking my head, I give the black bananas to my guest. And what happens next is something quite remarkable.

Using only her hands and teeth, Jewel bites off the end of each banana and squeezes each one in such a way that small rosette-shaped mounds soon appear all over her plate. They are very uniform and quite attractive. Then, gripping her spoon the way a small child might, she samples each little mound of soft banana. I have never witnessed anything like this before.

"You must be from California," I surmise.

"No, but I like soft food. Especially fruit."

"So what line of work are you in?'

"I do lots of things," she answers. And she quickly changes the subject and starts asking me questions.

"Raymondo, what were you doing in the river this morning?

And why did you have your pockets filled with rocks?"

I take a deep breath, preferring not to talk about it. But the stranger with the startling green eyes looks at me and will not stop staring until I say something.

"Now, first of all, my name is not 'Raymondo.' It's Raymond O. Knutson. But feel free to call me 'Ray.' I'm definitely not a 'Raymondo.' As you can see, I'm Norwegian. One-hundred percent! And about this morning, I made a mistake, Jewel. I thought I didn't want to live, but maybe I hadn't thought it through. But I tell you what, that ice-cold water sure woke me up. Guess I just needed a little jolt this morning.

"But the real question," I continue, "is what were *you* doing in the middle of the river at such an early hour? I didn't see anyone around when I went in, but suddenly there you were and then I was on the bank of the river in my underwear. How on earth did you manage to drag me to shore? How?"

The young woman smiles at me with her startling green eyes.

"The hard part was pulling off your shoes and pants. The rest was fairly easy."

To hide my embarrassment, I laugh a little. But I am still not satisfied with Jewel's explanation.

"Oh, this is good," Jewel says, as she finishes the last of her black banana rosettes.

"Well, since you like bananas so much, I have a banana story for you. You know, Ole and Lena were an old married couple who had never been on a train before. Right before they boarded, they bought a couple of bananas so they would have something to snack on. Well, the train got going and it chugged on and on. Ole got awful hungry and just as he took his first bite of the banana, the train went into a tunnel. It was one of those really long tunnels. And it was pitch-black inside. Now Ole leaned over and he said to his wife, *'Hav youu tried youur banana yet, Lena?'* She shook her head to show she wasn't hungry. *'Vell,'* Ole says to her, *'don't youu eat it! I took yuust one bite and I vent blind! Yah, Lena, I vent blind!'"*

I cannot keep from laughing as I tell the story. But after I finish, Jewel just looks at me and does not crack a smile. I am tempted to explain that "Ole and Lena" stories are often told in this part of the country. Perhaps most surprising of all, they are actually told by us Norwegian-Americans. I guess this shows we are so secure that we can poke a little fun at ourselves and even our sing-song accents. But Jewel, she still looks kinda lost and confused. I would sure hate to be a comedian and tell jokes to a whole room full of Jewels. Perhaps with this Jewel, I need to try something else.

"Just sit tight," I advise. "If you enjoy soft bananas, I've got a real treat for you. And it will warm us both up. You ever hear of *Rømmegrøt*? It's a porridge that is real soft and quite tasty. My Grandma Knutson used to make it from scratch. But I've got a package here that I bought at a little Scandinavian shop in downtown Fargo. The dry ingredients are pretty basic and include white flour, powdered milk, sugar—things like that. I just add some cold water and sour cream and heat it up. Oh, and I stir the heck out of it. You gotta do that. It burns easy if you're not paying attention. So just relax and get ready for some Norwegian *Rømmegrøt*. Okay?"

Jewel watches me for several minutes as I prepare the porridge. When it is done, I pour some of the thick white mixture into two bowls. For the crowning touch, I put a dollop of butter atop each bowl and generously sprinkle both portions with some cinnamon.

"Here it is," I say. "Give it a try and see what you think."

Jewel observes how I slowly stir the butter and cinnamon into my own portion. I blow on it before taking each spoonful and Jewel follows my every move.

But to my dismay, the young woman says nothing about the taste or the texture.

"I grew up on food like this," I explain. "We had cows on the farm, and so we always had lots of milk and cream. To me, this dish is real comfort food. But maybe a person has to grow up with it to truly appreciate it."

My guest still does not say a word, but she finishes her portion before I do. And she uses her fingers to clean out the bowl, and then she licks them off without apology. She does not have to tell me she likes the porridge. Sometimes, actions do speak louder than words.

I give Jewel a second helping of *Rømmegrøt,* and she soon finishes that portion as well. Then she grows very quiet.

"Is everything alright, Jewel? Did you not get enough to eat?"

She looks at me in an almost angry fashion. There is no mistaking that her mood has changed.

"Yes, that was tasty. And it took only a few minutes to prepare. Oh Raymondo, how could you have wanted to end your life, when you have things like this right at your fingertips? How could you have done what you tried to do this morning?"

Every time she says that darn 'Raymondo' name, I frown and want to set her straight. But to be honest, I am still enjoying the sweet and savory aftertaste of the sour cream porridge and thus have my mind on other things. My God, this *Rømmegrøt* is good, and it's not even the real thing. It was pre-packaged! No matter, I should have made some for myself before going into the river. Prisoners on death row get a last meal. Jesus and even that evil Judas both had a last supper. Come to think of it, the creamy *Rømmegrøt* would make a perfect last dish for anyone.

"Jewel," I finally confess, "I got some bad news last Thursday. The doctor told me I'm very ill. In fact, I've got a terminal condition. There's nothing modern medicine can do for me. I didn't want my demise to be a long, drawn-out affair. I went through all that with my poor wife Tillie. I was there for her and I was fine with that. But this time around, I wanted to take care of things myself. I wanted to do it my way. *My way,* you know."

"So that's why you wrote what you did on that stone?"

"Yes, and then you popped up out of nowhere and you saved

me. I guess I need to take that as some kind of sign. Maybe I need to rethink things."

"That's often a good idea, Raymondo. So tell me, when you re-think things, does it ever help to just get in the car and drive until you figure out what to do?"

"Oh yeah," I answer. "Before loading myself down with rocks and going into the river, I drove around for a couple of days think-ing about things. And then I decided to do what I did this morning."

Jewel laughs. "Maybe you need another person in the car to talk to and bounce ideas off of—before you reach any final conclusions."

I sense Jewel has something in mind. "Is there someplace you think we oughta go today?'

Jewel pauses and gives the matter some thought. With her right hand, she lightly rubs her chin. But it is her startling green eyes that make me wonder what exotic place she might want to visit. I am betting it will be a little town with a really unusual name—like Anamoose, Hoople, Omemee, Stirum, or Zap. Years ago, college kids from all over the country piled into their cars and did a "Zip to Zap." So maybe it will be Zap, North Dakota.

"Let's go to Wahpeton," she says.

"Wahpeton?" I repeat in disbelief. It is a small city that lies about sixty miles southeast of Fargo.

"Yes," Jewel responds. "I have a friend there. My visit shouldn't take too long. Maybe only a few minutes. Then we can head back here to Fargo. And we can talk along the way. Might be good for both of us. So what do you say, Raymondo?"

There's that darn name again. But now I am the one who is deep in thought.

It turns out that I have "this thing" about Wahpeton. In high school, our Fargo basketball team played the "Wahpeton Wops." Yes, that was their name. I don't think it was meant to be an ethnic slam. Most of the kids on the team had German or Norwegian names, and yet they proudly called themselves the 'Wops.' The

31

folks in Wahpeton probably thought the team's name sounded cute or something. It was back in the 1960s, before certain teams were pressured to change their names. There were some rather odd ones then. But here is what I am really getting at. Like the name or not, the "Wahpeton Wops" actually beat us. And the headline in the Fargo paper the next day wasn't too flattering. It took us guys a long time to live that one down. A basketball team from the big city of Fargo—whopped by the "Wahpeton Wops"!

Jewel just stares at me with those startling green eyes. She does not seem to even blink. Then her lips slowly curve into a slight but irresistable smile.

"Raymondo, do you want to go to Wahpeton?"

"Sure," I lie.

CHAPTER 4

After doing the breakfast dishes and finishing our laundry, I back my car out of the garage. Mrs. Gunderson is sweeping off the sidewalk and she manages to look my way at the same time. I wave, but she stares past me, trying to get a good look at the strange woman who is sitting at my right. Maybe Mrs. Gunderson is more than just curious. Maybe she's getting jealous.

Before heading to Wahpeton, Jewel asks me to swing through downtown Fargo. Evidently, she hasn't seen all the important sights. We take Broadway, one of the main streets that goes through the north side of town. Within only a few minutes, I direct Jewel's attention to two of the largest churches in Fargo. Each has a high, cross-tipped steeple and the churches are right across from each other. The two old buildings seem to be engaged in an eternal face-off. One is the Lutheran church that faces west and the other is the Catholic cathedral, which is oriented in the opposite direction.

"I just never feel right going into a Catholic church," I confess. "The minute you go in there, people are dipping their fingers in holy water and crossing themselves. Some even kiss their thumbs. And that's what they do when they first enter the church! There are always more little rituals and more surprises to come. So Tillie and me, we always went to different churches. After Sunday services, we would meet at the car and then go out to dinner. The church thing wasn't an ideal arrangement, but it worked alright. Sometimes, even when you love each other, you have to step back a little and give each other some space."

Now we approach a five-story, pale brick building on the west side of the street. I go real slow so that Jewel can see what I am talking about.

"That used to be the Powers Hotel," I say. "Peggy Lee actually performed in the hotel coffee shop back in the 1930s. That was before she became so famous. Her real name was Norma Deloris Egstrom, and she was born in Jamestown, North Dakota. When Peggy Lee performed here in Fargo, people could tell right away she was headed for stardom. She'd had a sad childhood, one that scarred her emotionally and even physically. Poor girl! Maybe that is what gave her voice such an unforgettable sound."

"Was she Scandinavian?" Jewel politely asks. I figure she wants me to know she is listening.

"Oh yeah," I answer. "Or maybe I should say 'Yah shure, ya betcha!' But yeah, I think Peggy Lee was half-Norwegian and half-Swedish. And she was all heart. No one could sing like her. When she passed away about fifteen years ago, it was like a little piece of a whole lot of us died with her. She was that special. I have several of her old albums. Tillie and me, we often listened to Peggy Lee. I hate to dance, but Tillie knew what to do. She would put on a Peggy Lee record, and that's how she got me to dance. Oh, that Tillie! And what a combination—my wonderful Tillie and the wonderful singing of Peggy Lee."

As we continue down Broadway, I also point out the historic Fargo Theatre and a small family restaurant that is on the corner across the street.

"It's probably the oldest pizza place in all of North Dakota," I say. "They still toss the pizza dough like in times past, and you can stand outside and watch them do it through the window. And once the pies are done, they cut the pizza into little squares rather than triangular pieces. My parents took me there on my twelfth birthday. That's when I tried my first real pizza. I still remember that day like it was yesterday. So every now and then, I go into that old restaurant. The smells and tastes and sounds are pretty much the same. You don't find that too often these days. It seems everything changes."

Jewel smiles and just lets me talk and complete my little tour "down memory lane."

"Yes," I go on, "everything changes. The other day I read that the most popular boy's name in Oslo, Norway, is now 'Mohammed.' Guess it isn't much different over here. Some of our young kids with the long Scandinavian surnames have first names like Dylan, Juanita, Liam, and Madonna. Our paper boy's name is Zappa Thorfinnson! Yeah, everything changes alright."

One of the reasons I agreed to this little outing was to get more information out of Jewel. I have already learned that with her, it's like pulling teeth. But when we get out on the highway, I start asking questions.

"What was your last name again?"

"I don't think I told you."

"Okay then, what's your last name?"

"Rhee."

"Rhee? So your name is Jewel Rhee—like the word 'jewelry'? Come on now! You really expect me to believe that?"

"Yes. That's my name."

As we approach the south edge of Fargo, we see large signs and buildings advertising "FIREWORKS." The signs do not just appear around the Fourth of July. They can be seen throughout the entire year, even when deep snow blankets nearly everything.

"So tell me, Jewel Rhee, were you born in Fargo?"

"No."

"So where are you from then?"

"Around."

"What do you do for a living?"

"Lots of things. I get by."

"Do you go into downtown Fargo much?"

"No, but when I do, I usually spend a few hours in the public library."

"You spend hours in the library? Are you homeless then?"

"No. I have a home."

"Well, do you have family in Fargo?"

"Yes, but we all kind of keep to ourselves."

"Oh," and I let out a sigh. "That's kinda how it is these days for a whole lot of people, isn't it? Everyone is so busy, and they just don't seem to have time for each other."

On the highway we see many trucks hauling huge loads of freshly harvested sugar beets. The beets look brown and dirty. It has always amazed me how big ugly beets can be turned into tiny crystals of pure white sugar. I have had several opportunities to tour the sugar factory in the nearby city of Moorhead, but I just never got around to it. Now I never will.

"Jewel," I continue. "Do you spend a lot of time on the river?"

"Yes."

"So tell me the truth. Am I the first person you had to de-pants and drag out of the river?"

Jewel laughs and looks out the car window. There are dark plowed fields that extend far into the western horizon. Every so often, long rows of bare cottonwoods and other trees can be seen.

Now my green-eyed passenger turns to me and gives me a taste of my own medicine.

"What does the 'O' in your name stand for?"

"Oskar. It's my middle name. Had a grandpa by that name."

"Were you born in Fargo?"

"No, I was born on a farm a few miles north of Fargo. But when people ask me where I'm from, I just say 'Fargo.' It's easier that way."

"Have you lived in the Fargo area all your life?"

"No, after taking some business classes at NDSU for a few years, I was footloose and free. So I moved out to Bismarck and got a job there. Started out working in a hardware store. And eventually I bought that store and lived in Bismarck for about twenty years. Then I moved back to Fargo and opened a hardware store in North Fargo. Kept it going until only a couple of years ago."

"Do you have any brothers or sisters?"

Innocent as it sounds, Jewel's question makes me pause before answering. I'm not sure how much I should say.

"Yeah. I've got an older brother. His name is Walt, and he and his wife Doris live in South Fargo. Their kids are all grown now."

"Do you see them much?'

"Not really. We only get together once or twice a year, maybe on Christmas or the Fourth of July. We're just not very close."

"Does your older brother know about your illness?"

"No."

"Don't you think you should tell him?"

"No!"

"Why not? He's your brother. Maybe he could be of some help."

"Yeah, he *could* be of some help. But that won't happen. Walt and me, we just never got along. Even as kids, he did all he could to beat me down and keep me down. It was mostly done behind the scenes, of course. Early on, I got the feeling that Walt just wanted me to die or get lost or something. I'm not being overly dramatic. Oh no. When we were still living on the farm, Walt and me had upstairs bedrooms across from each other. One night that old farmhouse caught on fire. Walt never woke me or helped me get out. My dad was in the hospital at the time, recovering from an appendectomy. So it was my mom who had to race up the stairs, wrap me in a quilt, and carry me outside. She saved me. We all stood there in the snow and watched our house burn down. Mom was in her nightgown and house shoes. She and I had to share that one quilt as we huddled together to keep warm. Walt just stood there staring at the fire. He was in his winter coat and snow boots, clutching both his coin collection and his favorite comics. That was Walt. He always looked out for himself. How do you figure a guy like that?"

I am thinking I have already said too much. But something compels me to go on.

"I think one of the reasons I never got into the Bible too much is that if you read just the first fifty pages or so, you'll see that younger brothers don't fare too well. Right off the bat, Cain gets jealous and kills his younger brother Abel. I guess Cain really hated Abel's guts. Then there's the story of Joseph the Dreamer. His eleven older brothers dislike him so much they won't even greet him. They plot to murder him, but then decide to make a little cash instead. So they sell him into slavery. And then they lie to their old man and tell him that Joseph is dead. Now, if you're a little guy who is black and blue from getting beaten up by an older brother, the Bible doesn't offer you much hope. The age-old message seems to be: 'Kid, you'd better invest in a good pair of sandals and run for your life!'"

"Were there ever any times when you and your brother did get along?"

"Mighty few," I answer. "When we were kids, we used to go fishing on the river, but we spent most of the time just staring ahead and watching our bobbers. We didn't catch many fish. I think even those fish could sense the tension in the air. So then we would put our fishing poles aside and go exploring on our own. We managed to keep a lot of distance between ourselves, even when we were supposed to be having fun.

"As I see it, older brothers are either protectors or predators. Walt was a classic case of the latter. When I left Fargo in the 1970s, it was mostly to get away from him and his bad vibes. Felt good to be on my own and not have to deal with the name-callings and the constant put-downs. Besides, I grew to like it out in Bismarck. It's different there. Different in a good way."

"But then you moved back to Fargo, right?"

"Yeah. By then, Walt was wheeling and dealing in real estate. And he lived on the far south side, where most of the newer homes were being built. When Tillie and me moved back, we found us a house on the far north side, in a nice quiet neighborhood close to the Red River."

"Did you intend to live so close to the river?"

"Well, when I saw that this one house was on a hill well above the river, I liked that. You know how the Red River floods nearly every year, don't you? The big floods of 1997 and 2009 were among the worst. You could practically throw out a fishing line from my back patio. Oh, those floods were a sight to see.

"The only real drawback to living in our part of town," I admit, "is that when a south wind blows in our direction, we can smell the sewage plant. That's when we have to hold our noses and close all the windows. I'll never forget that when Tillie and me first bought our house in North Fargo, Walt laughed and laughed. And he teased us with an old rhyme: *'By the sewer plant they lived, by the sewer plant they died. To perish there they did decide, so we'll call it sewer-cide!'* Yeah, that was what Walt thought of our choice of a place to live. But Tillie and me, we were real happy with the house. We especially liked being so close to the river and all the walking trails."

"Was Tillie from Fargo, too?"

"Oh, no. She was from western North Dakota. Tillie grew up on a small ranch on the Standing Rock Sioux Indian Reservation. Their place was southwest of the town of Fort Yates. Me, all I had to deal with in Fargo was parking tickets and buzzing mosquitos. Tillie, on the other hand, she grew up with bucking broncs and buzzing rattlesnakes. She used to tell people she came of age in the wild, wild West. In many ways, she did."

"Was Tillie a Native American?"

"No, but a lot of people thought she was. Even Walt thought so for a long time. He didn't realize a lot of non-Indians live on reservations. Tillie and me, we explained it a number of times. But Walt wasn't one to listen. He knew everything and I knew nothing. Tillie did have dark hair and real dark eyes. So I guess she looked kinda Indian. But actually she was one tough German-Russian, who was never afraid to speak her mind. Her family's last name was 'Rothfuss,' which translates to 'Red Foot.' In the 1930s, Tillie's parents changed their last name to 'Red Foot' to kind of blend in with the Sioux and get along better with them. Oh, that Tillie. She took real pride in the name and that's why she often wore red socks and red shoes. And she didn't care what anybody thought. She was the extreme opposite of me, but somehow we got along. Weird thing is, we took a real liking to each other soon after we met."

"So how did the two of you meet?"

"Well, when I first went to Bismarck in the 1970s, I would go to this little café near the hardware store where I worked. Tillie was a waitress there, and she wore red socks and red shoes. Sometimes, she even wore a red bow in her hair to match. I was fascinated by her. She didn't know me from Adam, but she always called me 'honey.' Once, she handed me a plate with a folded-over pastry on it. She told me I should try it, and it was 'on the house.' I asked what it was, and she said *Blachenda.'* Well, I pushed the plate away and wouldn't touch it. I was kinda disgusted. When she came back and saw that I didn't even try it, she demanded to know why. I told her I did not want to eat 'placenta.' Oh, how she laughed. She had to lie down in the booth there and hold her stomach. That's how hard she laughed. Soon everyone in the café heard what was going on, and they were looking at me and laughing. My God, I felt like crawling under the table.

"Eventually, Tillie stopped laughing and explained to me that 'Blachenda' was a German-Russian turnover filled with cooked pumpkin and spices. To save face, I finally did take a bite and soon I finished the whole thing. That night, Tillie and me, we went dancing. Oh, it was something to see her dance in those bright red shoes and red socks. She was so light on her feet. Yes, there we were, the shy Norwegian guy from Fargo and the high-stepping German-Russian girl from Standing Rock. What a pair we were.

"I think we both fell in love that same night. Soon after, we got married in a big, tipi-shaped Catholic church in Fort Yates. The hymns that were sung were in English, German, Latin, and even the Sioux language. Right behind that unusual-looking church was one of the strangest cemeteries I've ever seen. There were a lot of Indian gravestones with names like Fire Heart and Loans Arrow. But the German-Russians, they used these big iron crosses as grave markers. Some of them were real fancy, with lots of curlicues and other designs. Guess they were made by real blacksmiths. Many of Tillie's relatives and friends are buried in that cemetery. Oh, the whole place, it was so different from what I was used to seeing.

"Yeah, we got married in Fort Yates. Tillie's folks weren't too thrilled about their daughter marrying a Protestant from the eastern part of the state. And my folks weren't too happy about me hooking up with an outspoken Catholic gal from an Indian reservation out west. But Tillie and me, we didn't care. We had each other. And that's all that mattered to us. We knew love would get us through. Yeah, and it did. It sure did."

I glance over at Jewel and I see that she has turned away and is pretending to look out the car window at the outlying fields. But it looks to me like she is crying and using her long red hair to wipe away the tears.

CHAPTER 5

"So where does your friend live?" I ask my green-eyed mystery lady.

We have turned off the interstate and are approaching the city of Wahpeton.

"I'm supposed to meet her on the north end of town—by the giant catfish. I'll only be a few minutes."

I stop at a gas station to fill up on fuel and to get some directions. Two men inside the station laugh when I inquire about the giant catfish.

"You mean the 'Big Wahpper?'" one of them teases. "Oh, you'll see him alright. Can't miss him."

A few minutes later, I park the car only a short distance from the Red River. Sure enough, there is a huge fiberglass catfish that must be about forty feet long. Its white mouth is open and its gray, blue, and silver colors glisten in the midday sun.

Seeing my interest, Jewel tells me to get a closer look while she seeks out her friend. I watch Jewel as she heads off toward some trees along the river. What is it about this green-eyed woman and rivers?

Half an hour later, after examining every inch of the "World's

Largest Catfish," I return to the car and wait. I worry that maybe all of this was not such a good idea. What if Jewel is a drug trafficker and she's doing a pick-up or a drop-off? And using me and my car to do it?

Just as I am about to take out my cell phone and call the police, Jewel appears. She is red-faced and out of breath.

"Are you alright?" I ask. "Did you find your friend?"

"Yes," Jewel answers. But she looks all around as if she is being watched. "We can go now."

"Don't you want to get a close look at the giant catfish?"

"No, I've seen my share of big catfish. There are a lot of them in this part of the river."

As we head south into downtown Wahpeton, I pull into a fast food place where we can get a bite to eat and use the restroom. I order a chicken sandwich and onion rings and a coffee. Jewel looks all around and then asks for some black bananas and *Rømmegrøt*. The eyes of the young girl behind the counter grow enormous. She looks at me as if she expects me to interpret.

"My friend's from out of town," I explain. "Could you make her a large banana milk shake? And maybe get her a double cheeseburger with the works, some French fries, and an apple sauce?"

When I bring all the food to the table, Jewel looks a little disappointed. But she soon samples everything except for the cheeseburger.

"Are you a vegetarian?"

Jewel ignores the question and makes considerable noise as she finishes the banana milkshake. When she holds up the plastic container to lick out the last drops, I notice an unusually large gold ring on her middle finger. It looks expensive and has three interwoven strands.

"That's a beautiful ring," I comment. "I hadn't even noticed it before."

"My friend Crystal gave it to me. That's why I needed to see her today."

Her friend Crystal? Now I am really getting worried. Two women named Jewel and Crystal? They are probably involved in some kind of international jewelry-smuggling operation. We are not that far from the Canadian border. Who is this green-eyed stranger anyhow?

As we make our way out of town, I am so lost in my thoughts that I somehow find myself on the far south side of Wahpeton. We pass an old cemetery and Jewel asks me to stop.

"Could we get out and walk around a bit? Maybe I drank that milkshake too fast. I'm feeling a little shaky myself."

"But we don't need to stop at an old graveyard. This one looks like it hasn't been used for years. Kinda gives me the creeps. Surely we can find a nice park with a restroom up ahead."

"No," Jewel protests. "This old cemetery is fine. I like these places and I visit them all the time. Besides, this is a cemetery I haven't seen before."

Soon we are walking in the graveyard and looking at the tombstones. Most of them face west and one of the older markers has a six-pointed star, but the inscription is almost impossible to read. Jewel seems fascinated and stops to read and study many of the grave markers.

Within a few minutes, we stand before a rather unusual memorial. It is a tall gray obelisk that is actually the rough-hewn sculpture of a broken mast, one covered with carved ropes and chains. The legend at the bottom of the memorial hints of a freak accident that killed two circus workers more than a century ago. Jewel is intrigued by the obelisk and examines it from every angle.

"Poor guys," I say. "They were probably a couple of farm kids who wanted to see the world. So they joined the circus and went from town to town. Doubt if they got paid much and they probably worked their tails off. Way back, when Walt and me were kids, our parents took us to the big show one summer. The circus drew such a large crowd that all the spectators could barely squeeze into the tent. Walt was supposed to hold my hand, but we got separated.

"I was only five at the time. I got pretty scared and started crying. Right before the big show began, a trapeze artist took me by the hand and she walked me into the middle of the ring. She got the audience's attention and then asked if anyone there had lost a little boy named 'Raymond.' As my folks got up and hurried to claim me, they noticed another couple from the other side of the tent coming to claim me as well. When that couple saw my folks, they quickly turned back and disappeared. For a long time afterward, my parents talked about that couple. Would they have come and taken me, if my folks had happened to be outside the tent looking for me? Guess we'll never know."

Jewel now kneels in front of the monument and reads aloud the names and dates. When she gets up and heads back to the car, she is humming to herself.

It takes us a few minutes to get on the interstate and head north to Fargo.

All of a sudden, Jewel begins to sing. Hers is a crystal-clear soprano voice that resonates throughout the whole car.

> It was back in the summer of 1897
> When the big circus came to town.
> Lightning, it flashed down from heaven,
> Now two circus workers, they sleep underground.
> Aye, two circus workers, they sleep underground.

"Jewel," I say, "you've got quite a voice. And you composed that little tune within the last few minutes?"

"Like I said before, I often visit cemeteries," Jewel admits. "It's amazing how little can be said on a stone. Yet the words convey so much feeling and meaning."

"Have you composed any other songs?" I ask. I really want to hear her voice again.

Jewel tilts her head back and soon I am serenaded with one song after another.

Herman lived for eighty-seven years.
His wife Mavis lived but sixteen less.
Oh, do not shed for them any tears.
Rejoice that they're both at rest.
Aye, rejoice that they're both at rest.

Young Taylor was a soldier brave.
He fought and he died overseas.
Now Taylor sleeps in a hallowed grave,
All bedecked with lovely leaves.
Aye, all bedecked with lovely leaves.

Robert was a rich lawyer, 'tis true.
For his wealth, many in town did yearn.
Robert did litigate and he did sue.
Now Robert rests in a simple urn.
Aye, now Robert rests in a simple urn.

Baby Amanda, baby mild,
You did not make it to a year.
Baby Amanda, baby mild,
You'll always be our baby dear.
Aye, you'll always be our baby dear.

"Those songs are terribly sad," I say. "Hearing you sing them is really something. But they are so sad. Maybe you should go to some street fairs or NDSU tailgate parties, so you have some happier material to work with? Not sure how many of those epitaph-songs I could listen to before I get pretty depressed and start filling my pockets with rocks again. You're much too young to be singing about dead people and death. Much too young."

I look over at Jewel and she simply stares ahead, as if she is fixated on all the white center stripes that we are passing on the highway. She probably thinks they symbolize coffins or something like that. My passenger seems to be in a bit of slump. I need to get her mind off cemeteries and death. And I know just the place.

CHAPTER 6

We are still on the interstate, but I have turned the car completely around and we are heading south again. We pass the Wahpeton exit and I aim the car in the direction of South Dakota. I need to cheer up Jewel, and so I figure it's time for a little Scandinavian culture.

"You know," I begin, "when Ole was a kid, he didn't do so well in Sunday school. He had a hard time remembering things from out of the Bible. It was such a big book, you know. After he got married, Lena sat him down and she said: '*Ole, youu must read yur Bible! Everyting youu need to know is in dat book. Youu'll see. Tell youu vhat—I'll gif youu a whole year to finish it. Okay?*' Well, one year later, that Lena, she quizzed Ole to see if he really read the whole Bible. She decided to start with a real easy question. '*So, Ole, vhat did youu tink of Saint Paul?*' Ole was awful nervous and he paused a bit before answering. He hated quizzes. '*Vell,*' Ole finally said, '*I saw dat name Saint Paul a lot in dat big Bible. But ya know, I dident see a single vord about Minneapolis! Yah, it makes youu kinda vunder, dussent it?*'"

Jewel looks at me as if there is more to come. But I just steel myself and repeat the words "*Yah, it makes youu kinda vunder, dussent it?"*

A short while later, I pull into the parking lot of the Prairie Mountain Casino. There is indeed a high hill close to the casino and I'm pretty sure it was not there originally. It's about fifty feet high and is covered with big rocks and lots of evergreens. With so much flat prairie surrounding it, the big hill really stands out. And it sure gets the attention of any motorists who have grown weary of the monotonous prairie landscape.

The parking lot is full of cars and trucks and buses. It seems there are always a lot of vehicles around. This place is open even on Thanksgiving, Christmas, and Super Bowl Sunday. In fact, I think it is open every day and every hour of the entire year.

I have not been to this Indian casino in at least a couple of years. Tillie always liked to come to this gaming spot. She would play the slot machines and try her hand at blackjack and roulette. After a few hours, we would eat at the big buffet, where they seemed to have more than enough of everything. Less often, we would take in a live show and listen to a comedian or a Country-Western band perform.

Truth is, I never much cared for bingo or Las Vegas or Indian casinos. Tillie, on the other hand, enjoyed these places immensely. When we won a little money and came out ahead, Tillie was ecstatic. On the nights we walked out of an Indian casino after almost losing our shirts, Tillie would say: "Well, at least we had some fun, didn't we, Raymond? And maybe we helped out the tribe a little." Boy, did we ever.

I think one of the reasons Tillie liked this casino so much was that everyone who worked here knew her. When she came through the doors, the employees would gather around and joke with her. The Indian women would hug her and compliment her on her latest choice of footware. In fact, they called her "Tillie Red Shoes." And me? Well, I was "that guy with Tillie Red Shoes." I have to admit that a lot of this was my fault. I just wasn't as huggable and outgoing as Tillie. Instead of driving to an Indian casino, I preferred to stay at home and watch a football game or a good documentary about World War II. A night like that certainly was a whole lot cheaper.

When Jewel and I get inside the Prairie Mountain Casino, she looks like she has landed on the moon and is taking her first steps. Jewel is intrigued by everything: the red carpets, the neon lights, the artwork, the mix of sounds, the smell of popcorn and hot dogs, the trays of soft drinks and alcoholic beverages, the cashiers working in cage-like structures, even the baskets of complimentary matchbooks and scented hand wipes. Jewel turns around and around to study it all. I am even tempted to say: "Calling from the Earth to the Moon, calling from the Earth to the Moon." Instead, I just let Jewel soak it all in like a thirsty space traveler might do.

Now I show my guest some of the slot machines Tillie liked to play. There are machines with animated video scenes of charging buffalo, galloping stallions, screaming eagles, squawking parrots, roaring lions, purring cats, and even dancing leprechauns. But the slot machine that Jewel seems really drawn to is the one with a woman who swims underwater with tropical fish and sea turtles. Tillie used to play this same machine, and one night she did so for five hours straight. I sat behind her, bored out of my mind. But every half an hour or so, I cheered her on and silently prayed that she would win at least a modest jackpot so we could head home and go to bed.

Jewel stares at the large video screen showing the underwater woman. I had never noticed it before, but the woman in the video also has long red hair and green eyes. Jewel obviously notes the resemblance, and she grins at me to make sure I see the connection. She even taps on the glass screen to get the red-haired woman's attention.

I coax Jewel to sit down in front of the machine and to play it for a while. I slip a twenty-dollar bill into the machine and show

Jewel how to press the fifty-cents button at the far left. I also take out my old player's card from my wallet and put the card into the machine. This way, while Jewel plays, I can at least get some points on my card. When a player accumulates enough points, these can be redeemed for food, lodging, and even gasoline.

Jewel hits the slot machine button again and again. Each time she does, the whole scene changes and the underwater woman swims back and forth. When three or more identical images appear side by side on the screen, there is a small payout. Jewel is enjoying herself so much that I slip in another twenty-dollar bill. Now I'm no show-off, and I sure don't want people to think I'm a big spender. I'm not. Putting a twenty-dollar bill into one of these machines is like sticking my fingers into the fast-moving blades of a power lawnmower. But I do want Jewel to have a little fun and get her mind off cemeteries and all those epitaphs. Maybe this gambling thing will do it. And maybe she'll even sing a happy song or two on the way home. Now that would be worth something.

After I remind Jewel to keep playing only the fifty-cents button, I look around for an ATM to get some more cash. I certainly don't plan to spend it all at this casino. But I do need to have some money in my billfold for when we head home. There is a long line of people at the ATM, but finally I get to the front and withdraw a few bills and get my receipt.

About fifteen minutes later, when I get back to Jewel, I see that she is still playing the same machine. She has even managed to hit a few bonuses. But I notice that in her excitement, Jewel's hand has wandered to the far right and she is playing the maximum amount button. That one is five dollars a hit! Just as I rush in to stop her from continuing to press the wrong button, something happens. The lights flash, loud music plays, and a message on the screen informs us that Jewel has won a $25,548.50 progressive jackpot!

$25,548.50! I cannot believe my eyes. Tillie and me, we never won anything even close to this amount. I look at Jewel and she is more excited by the lights and the music than the huge jackpot win. People behind her congratulate her and several touch her hair and shoulders, as if they want some of the good luck to rub off on themselves. Seeing Jewel sit there, smiling and laughing, oh, it is a moment to savor and remember.

Ah, but the magic and the excitement are short-lived. The casino manager and two other casino employees soon stand before us and ask if Jewel is "Tillie Knutson." That name, after all, is the one on the player's card that was in the machine at the time of the jackpot win. I check my billfold and sure enough, I took out Tillie's card instead of my own. Both of our cards look exactly the same, except for the names that appear in small letters at the bottom of each card. I had neglected to look more closely!

The grim-faced casino manager tells us that since the person who won the jackpot was using "a dead person's player card," the big win will have to be declared null and void. He repeats that for any jackpot payout to be valid, the person who wins must be *alive* and have his or her own player's card in the machine at the exact time of the big win. I want to argue, but I notice that several hefty security guards now stand behind the manager and the two other casino employees. We are definitely outnumbered and outgunned. Besides, I prefer to spare myself and Jewel any further embarrassment.

As we head out the big glass doors of the casino, the manager stops us and hands Jewel a blanket emblazoned with geometric designs and a full-color image of the prairie mountain that evidently gave the casino its name. Jewel accepts the consolation prize and caresses it to show how much she appreciates the gift. The manager then looks at me and hands me several coupons for free meals, gasoline, and two nights lodging in the casino's honeymoon suite.

"I'm sorry how things went today," the manager tells me. "I truly am. But we have our rules here. And I want you to know I remember Tillie and we all miss her and we offer you our condolences. We give these things to you and your new wife in honor of 'Tillie Red Shoes.' She was not just a dear friend. She was like a sister to many of us."

I am kinda choked up, but also too embarrassed to try to explain everything. I simply nod and motion to Jewel that we should go to the car and do so quickly. Some young people in the front lobby recognize us and point and laugh. They probably think we are big-time hustlers and go from one casino to another using dead people's player cards.

Talk about peaks and valleys! One minute we're winners and have scored a big jackpot. The next minute we look like hustlers and imposters. Maybe the blanket that Jewel got is for the both of us to cover our heads in shame.

To complicate matters, Jewel now motions that she needs to use "the little room" before we skedaddle to the parking lot. She pushes the Indian blanket against my chest and I soon find myself pacing back and forth outside the ladies' room. The minutes pass by and they seem like hours. I keep my head down so that no one else will recognize me. When Jewel finally returns, her face is dripping wet. I just hand her the blanket and I ask no questions.

When we are back in the car and on the highway heading toward Fargo, I look over at Jewel to check if she's alright. Poor girl! And here I wanted to introduce her to a world of fun and games and entertainment. Things sure didn't go too well.

Draped in her new Indian blanket, Jewel has her eyes closed. I notice that she has kicked off her shoes, just the way Tillie always did when we went on a long car ride. Jewel has her arms outside the blanket and her hands rest on her lap. And the three-strand ring on her finger shines brightly.

CHAPTER 7

My passenger groans in her sleep and does not rest long. She awakens just as we pass the little town of Galchutt. My brother Walt once dated a girl from Galchutt. When they were together, he deliberately mispronounced her name and even the name of her hometown, so that it sounded like the droppings of a certain sea-bird. After they broke up, she sent Walt a pretty nasty letter. Above his name and address she wrote "TO WALDO THE ...." And then that Galchutt gal let loose with every off-color term imaginable. She sure got the last word. Even the postman knew it.

Jewel hums to herself and I'm hoping she will sing more of her songs. I don't much care for the cemetery stuff, but I do like the sound of her voice.

"Did you and Tillie have any children?" Jewel quietly asks.

Well, she beat me to it again. And here I was, preparing to ask her more questions.

"No," I answer. "Tillie wasn't able to have children. In our younger years we talked about adopting a little boy and a little girl. But we didn't think it would be fair to them. At the time, we both needed to work full-time and we didn't want the kids to spend most of their time at a babysitter's house. So Tillie came up with a great idea. We decided to send a big donation a few times each year to a well-known children's hospital back east.

"You know," I continue, "I have a large photo album at home with color photos of some of the kids we helped over the years. When friends stopped by the house and proudly showed us pictures of their children and grandchildren, Tillie brought out the big photo album. She showed them photos of the many children we helped. She knew their names and she even corresponded with some of them. They were kids of every color and religion, and they lived all over the world. Tillie loved each and every one."

"And did *you* love Tillie—I mean, *really* love her?"

I am taken aback by the boldness of her question. But then I remember that the person who is asking is a bit different. She prefers black bananas and old cemeteries. I have to cut her some slack, maybe a whole lot of slack.

"Tillie and me, we had something very special. And that was despite our being the complete opposites of each other. Yet we fell in love and through all the ups and downs of our years together, we never fell out of love. These days, with so many divorces, that's saying something.

"You know, on the day we got married, that ceremony in the tipi-shaped church really threw me for a loop. I felt like a fish out of water. At times, I could hardly breathe. My God, I had never set foot in a Catholic church before. And yet there I was, getting married in a church shaped like an Indian tipi! But the minister, or rather the priest, he read something out of the Bible. Then I felt a little better. At least those Catholics with all their holy water and incense, they did use the Bible. And that was something I grew up with. Now I didn't really study it, but there was always a Bible in our home. The priest, he read a passage that was all about love. And as he read the words, Tillie looked up at me with those beautiful dark eyes. And she smiled and squeezed my hand."

"Do you remember what the priest said?"

"Yes. And I have thought about that passage many times since. It goes something like this: 'In the end, there are only three things that last—faith, hope, and love, and the greatest of these is love.'

"At that moment, I knew that what Tillie and me had would last. It was love. But then, as we headed out of that tipi-shaped church, all the wedding guests sure brought us back down to earth in a hurry. They pelted us with kernels of corn. Not little grains of white rice, mind you. But big, hard, multicolored kernels of corn. It was Indian country, after all. So they pelted us with Indian corn!

"And as we went down the steps, Tillie lifted her long white wedding gown just a bit, and we all could see her red stockings and red bridal shoes. Oh, that Tillie! What an amazing woman. When she was born, the angels must have thrown away the mold. There was no one else like her. I was fortunate just having the time with her that I did.

"Now don't get me wrong. As I said before, my life with Tillie wasn't perfect. Into every life a little rain—and sometimes a few mighty big hailstones—must fall. Sure, Tillie and me, we had our days. Every married couple has to weather a storm or two. Maybe it all happens just to keep life interesting.

"I still haven't figured out this thing called 'life.' Not sure if I ever will. You see, life is just too big and too complicated. A little ant can take on a great big watermelon, but that little ant can't take on the whole world. There are limits, you know. Maybe we humans should be content with the watermelon that life has rolled our way. And who knows?—maybe we can have our watermelon and eat it, too.

"I'm no philosopher, but this is how I see it: We humans get born, we grow up, we get hitched, we work hard, we get old, and then we croak. If, in between any of those different stages, we experience some real love or some real happiness . . . well, that's when I'd say we're blessed. Truly blessed."

I look over at Jewel and suddenly realize what she is doing.

She is getting me to open up and talk in order to avoid any of my questions.

"What happened to Tillie?" my young passenger asks. Her startling green eyes tell me she really wants to know.

I don't want to talk about it. And I'm not sure if I can. But I realize I need to finish my story before asking Jewel about hers.

"Tillie died a little over a year ago. It was breast cancer and it got pretty bad toward the end. Tillie was tough and even when she was in a lot of pain, she tried not to let on. And she hated taking pain pills. She said they threw her off and that there were some really bad side effects.

"For a time, Tillie was in the hospital in Fargo where the doctors and nurses could monitor her closely. But with all the interruptions and noisy equipment, she couldn't get much rest.

"One day, my brother Walt stopped by the hospital. In no time at all, he was telling us about his latest real estate deals. I somehow managed to change the subject, and then Walt decided to impress us with his medical knowledge. He said that Tillie should have given birth to at least a couple of children because when women do not have any children, they often get breast cancer. He claimed it was Nature's way of taking revenge. I could see how hurt and uncomfortable Tillie was getting. I told Walt to shut up and just let Tillie rest. He left in quite a huff and later he told his wife and some other people that I was rude and threw him out of the hospital room. And yet he had taken time out of his busy schedule to go see Tillie, but had been mistreated!

"Well, after Walt left the hospital that day, I felt so bad for Tillie. She had enough to deal with without Walt's stupidity. Tillie looked at me and she said she had always hoped Walt and me would get along better someday. But now she wasn't sure. And she told me, 'Maybe there's no hope for him, Ray. He's got his head up where the sun don't shine. And yet he's your only brother and you have to deal with him. Poor Ray!'

"Yeah, that was Tillie. There she lay, suffering and dying in a hospital bed. And she felt sorry for me—not for herself, but for me. I took her home shortly after that, so she could get some real rest and we also could screen who came to visit.

"After that, Tillie, she had good days and bad days. Oh, she would smile and even joke with me, but a few minutes later, I would hear her behind a closed door crying out in pain. Tillie told me many times that it was quite enough for one person to suffer. Two people shouldn't have to go through it all. But we did. And, bad as it was, I'm glad that we did. I think that's what love is all about."

A few minutes pass and neither of us says a word. We are approaching the outskirts of Fargo.

"I have one more song to share," Jewel announces. She tilts her head back and once again the car resonates with the fullness of her soprano voice:

> *A pair of shoes on a tombstone,*
> *Bright red amidst all the gray.*
> *In her dreams Tillie is never alone,*
> *For she's dancing with Ray every day.*
> *Aye, she's dancing with Ray every day.*

I am an old man who seldom cries in front of other people. But I am shaking so much that I have to grab hold of the steering wheel with both hands. And I weep so hard that I have to pull over to the side of the highway. I am sad and angry and stunned all at the same time.

Who is this person in my car? How did she know I had red shoes engraved on the gray headstone that marks the final resting place of Tillie and me? The green-eyed woman sees me crying and she offers no explanation and no apology. She just stares at me. My God in heaven, who is this woman?

CHAPTER 8

When we get back to Fargo, I am still wondering about Jewel. As I pull into the driveway, I remember something from my childhood. My parents often would pick up my Grandma Knutson and take her with us when we went on shopping trips. Then we would bring her home with us and we would eat lunch together. Even before we got out of the car and headed into the house with our groceries, Grandma Knutson would say, *"Borte bra, men hjemme best."* I must have heard those words nearly a hundred times or more. It was a Norwegian expression that meant something like "Home sweet home."

At the moment, I'm not quite sure about the wisdom of that old saying. Even though I am back home, things don't feel so sweet. They certainly don't feel right. I even hesitate for a moment to let Jewel back into the house. I had concerns about her before, and now I really have mixed feelings. Something about her just doesn't feel right.

Once Jewel and I are in the house, I show her where to sit down on the couch in the living room. After I pile up some large couch cushions to her right and left, I carry in a large wooden chair from the kitchen. I sit right in front of Jewel so that our knees are almost touching. I have her boxed in for a reason. It is my turn to ask the questions.

"Now, how did you know about the red shoes engraved on our headstone—Tillie's and mine? How?"

I do not even ask Jewel if she happened to notice the bolts and screws that were engraved on my side of the tombstone. They were supposed to represent the hardware store that I had for so many years. Now that I think about it, when people see the bolts and screws, they'll probably think "gee, that guy must have had some screws loose." Oh, this symbols stuff, it can be mighty tricky.

"Well," I repeat, "how'd you know what was on our headstone?"

Jewel looks apprehensive. She seems to sense my seriousness, as well as my frustration.

"I saw the marker in a cemetery not far from here a few weeks ago," she tells me. "It really stood out. But I didn't put it all together until you told me about Tillie and her red shoes and how she loved to dance. I'm glad I know the story now. It's very touching."

I stare into her startling green eyes and ask her as directly and firmly as I can.

"Who are you? Tell me the truth now. Who are you?"

"But I already told you. My name is Jewel Rhee."

"Do you have any kind of identification with a picture or something?"

"No, not with me. Why do you ask?"

"Because I need to know who you really are. With your interest in black bananas and cemeteries, I think I have it figured out now. You're Death!"

"Death? Would Death have rescued you from drowning this morning? That doesn't make any sense."

"Are you an angel sent from heaven?"

"Hardly," Jewel replies. "Please stop this."

But I do not let up on the questioning. I need answers.

"What are you?"

"What do you mean?'

"Are you human?"

Tears fill the young woman's green eyes. She struggles to get up to leave, but I continue to box her in, in order to get at least some basic information out of her. More tears roll down her cheeks and she brushes them away with both hands.

"Jewel, are you from out there, from beyond the stars?"

"So now you're thinking I came out of some spaceship? No, I am not a space alien, Raymondo."

There's that darn name again. And for the umpteenth time, I have to set her straight.

"I am not Raymondo! My name is Raymond. You know that."

Jewel now makes an effort to push me back and she gives it a good try. But she is not going anywhere.

"Ray, this is all pretty silly. I need to leave. It'll be dark soon."

"Interesting. So you need to be gone by dark. Are you a ghost?"

"Ghosts aren't afraid of the dark."

"How do you know about ghosts?"

"I know about a lot of things, Ray. And believe me, you don't want to hear about most of them. It's better for you not to know."

"Now what does that mean?'

"It's complicated. And I can't say too much."

"But that's my point here. You're not telling me much."

"Then that's going to have to be the way it is, Ray. If I tell you certain things, it might put you in harm's way."

"In harm's way? Are you dealing drugs or maybe working with an international smuggling ring?"

I raise my eyebrows and stare at her big gold ring to emphasize the point.

For a long time, the young woman looks down at the three-strand ring on her middle finger. When she finally looks up, she seems to have a change of heart.

"Ray, can I ask you something?"

"No. It's my turn to ask the questions."

"Please, Ray. Just one question. Please."

"Okay. Give it your best shot."

"This morning, as you were going into the river, you said some words. It was something that rhymed. What exactly did you say, Ray?"

It's hard to believe that I walked into the river earlier this morning. It seems like days ago, not hours. But then I remember what Jewel is asking about and I have to laugh to myself a little.

"Funny you should ask about that. It was a little rhyme that my Grandma Knutson taught me when we would cross over rivers. Nothing more. Just some nonsense words."

"Are you sure? If they were just nonsense words, why then did you say them as you were about to drown yourself in the river?"

"I'm not really sure. Those words just came back to me. It was like instinct or something."

"What were the words, Ray? Tell me the words."

Jewel looks straight at me and patiently waits for me to recite the verse. I feel kind of silly, but then I close my eyes for a few seconds and I say the words:

Nix, nix, nix!
Calm the rivers,
Calm the cricks.
No more troubles,
No more tricks.
Nix, nix, nix!

Jewel listens with rapt attention. Her green eyes grow large and bright as I emphasize the last three words. And her face glows.

"I didn't think anyone remembered," Jewel whispers. "That's an English version of something the old Scandinavians used to say before they crossed a river. You see, in times past, people didn't just cross a river and think nothing of it. Crossing a river could be very dangerous. If you were about to ford a stream or a river, you had to do so with respect. A river was not just a river. It was the domain of invisible but very powerful entities. These ancient entities needed to be acknowledged and appeased. And there could be serious consequences for human arrogance and improper behavior.

"Did your grandmother ever advise you to grab onto metal as you said the verse?" Jewel asks.

"No," I reply. "But wait a minute—she did tell us to touch the roof of the car when we said it. If it was summer and the window was down, we would reach up and touch the outside roof of the car."

"And the roof was made of metal, right?" Jewel asks with a nod and a smile. "I thought so. In ancient times, when people said a verse like that, they would grab hold of their sword or their axe or an iron wagon-part. It was a way of protecting themselves doubly well. But it is the verse that is most important. Touching metal simply was to provide extra protection."

As I listen to Jewel's voice, I cannot help thinking of my Grandma Knutson and the stories she used to tell me at bedtime. Whenever Walt beat on me, Grandma would come into my bedroom and tell me those stories to comfort me and get me to stop crying.

"You know, my grandmother, she often spoke about all kinds of spirits, trolls, and other mysterious beings. She had different names for them, but most of the time she just lumped them altogether and referred to them as 'the *Huldre Folk*—the Unseen Ones.' I loved to hear her tell those stories. Her eyes would light up and she would use her hands as she talked.

"Sometimes Grandma would cup her hands together and tell me there was a little flame inside them. She would bend down and peer inside her cupped hands. And she'd blow upon them real gentle-like. I never did see the flame that Grandma talked about.

"Once, however, Grandma Knutson asked me to touch her

cupped hands. And they did feel kinda hot. I'm still not sure what that cupped hands ritual was all about. It was but one of many things I didn't fully understand. Maybe I was just too young.

"How I wish I could go back in time and talk to Grandma again. Maybe I could get some answers. But that's not possible. I reckon Grandma took most of her secrets to the grave.

"There was another ritual, one that I did understand. Each evening, after Grandma Knutson was done talking to me, she would warn me never to say a word to our Lutheran minister about the *Huldre Folk* or the things she told me. Not a single word."

Jewel nods and smiles. Then she puts an upright index finger to her lips and lightly taps her mouth. After telling some stories, Grandma Knutson sometimes did that as well.

CHAPTER 9

Even though I still have Jewel boxed in on my living room couch, she continues to ask me questions. However does she do it, constantly distracting me and getting me to talk? Maybe she is a secret government agent and does interrogations. If so, she's pretty good.

"Ray, did your Grandma Knutson ever talk to you about the *Nøkk?*"

"She might have. I can't quite recall. I grew up speaking mostly English, so all those Old Country terms were kinda hard for me to sort out and remember."

"Strange," Jewel says, "how your grandmother kept their name alive in that old verse of yours. Like when she would say '*nix, nix, nix.*' The pronunciation was off a bit. But she was calling upon the *Nøkk,* one of the spirits of the water. I just couldn't believe it when I heard you saying that verse in the river this morning. Was I ever surprised."

"So are you a *Nøkk?* Is that like a mermaid or something?"

Jewel throws back her head and laughs. She finally seems to be enjoying this little question-and-answer session.

"Mermaid!" she exclaims. "Mermaids, Sirens, the Lorelei—they sure seem to get a lot of attention. But I think you watch too much television, Ray. It would be better for you to go to the library and do some real research."

"Like you sometimes do?" I ask.

"Yes, I do a lot of reading at the library. There they have books and films about nearly everything. I even study the dictionary. And it is very quiet there and nobody disturbs me."

"Okay, Jewel, I'll admit something. I'm kinda fascinated by all this stuff about the *Huldre Folk*. I do want to know more, so play along with me and humor an old man like myself. Okay?"

I back up and give Jewel a bit more breathing room. I want her to feel at ease as I continue asking questions.

"In my grandma's verse, she would say *'no more troubles, no more tricks.'* That seems to tell me that the *Nøkk* can be mischievous and even harmful. So is a *Nøkk* a bad spirit that can hurt people?"

"Again, it's complicated, Ray. Remember what you said about brothers—that they can be either protectors or predators? The same might be said of the various types of the so-called *Huldre Folk*. Some are quite kind and they protect. But others do anything but protect. The male *Nøkk*, for example, can be very conniving and very dangerous."

"So then, how does one tell the difference?"

Jewel sits up and uses both her hands as she talks. I am not sure where all this is going, but I follow along just the same.

"Telling the difference is also complicated. But believe me, the difference is very real and sometimes you don't realize it until it's too late. That's why the old verse of your grandmother's is so interesting. A verse like that can repel the power of the male *Nøkk* just by calling out his name. Your ancestors knew how to do more than bake bread and make *Rømmegrøt*. They knew how to protect themselves in a very dangerous and unpredictable world."

"When I was younger," I admit, "I was really into all of this. But my parents and my brother Walt were not interested at all. I think

Mom and Dad were kind of ashamed of the Norwegian accents and all the Old Country traditions. They tried hard to fit in and be accepted as Americans. My brother Walt thought the Norwegian stuff was a bunch of crap and he would make fun of me when I tried to talk about it. But my Grandma Knutson, she's the one who told me so many stories. Once, I asked her where all the old spirits and mysterious beings came from. Her answer really surprised me."

"What did she say, Ray?"

"Grandma Knutson claimed it was all right there in the Bible. When I got older, I searched and searched. And I knew better than to ask a Lutheran minister. Grandma had warned me about that. I kept looking, but I never found any explanation in the Bible. Then again, I had to remind myself that the Bible wasn't written by a bunch of Norwegians. So maybe Grandma was mistaken or a bit confused."

"No, Ray, I don't think your grandma was mistaken or confused. In terms of the old ways, she sounds like she was quite knowledgeable and respectful. And her insights strike me as rather luciferous."

Usually, when I hear a big word that I don't know, I just pretend to understand it. I think a lot of us do that. We just let it go. But not this time.

"Say, what was that word you just used, Jewel?"

"Sorry, I guess I do spend too much time in the library. It was just an old-fashioned term. I didn't mean to sound ostentacious. Whoops—did I do it again?"

"That word that you said before," I respond. "It sounded like 'luciferous.' As in 'Lucifer'? Who uses a word like 'luciferous'? My God, Jewel, are you a devil or something like that? Are you?"

The green-eyed Jewel Rhee now grows very silent. She is quiet for a long time, and then deftly steers things in a different direction.

"Regarding your grandma and the Bible—I think I can help

you, Ray. Do you happen to keep a Bible in your home?"

I hesitate to get up and allow Jewel the freedom to make a dash for the door. But my old Bible is not far away. It is in an end table drawer here in the living room.

Soon I hand the big, leather-bound book to Jewel, but she declines to take it in her hands. She motions for me to use the Bible and I find the gesture puzzling.

"Okay, Jewel, what should I be looking for?"

"Turn to the back and find Revelations. And then look for the part that tells about a great war in the heavens."

Uff da! I am not much of a Bible scholar. I fear I am more like the Ole character in my stories, the Ole who isn't too familiar with the Bible. Besides, there is a reason this holy book is kept in an end table drawer and not on my nightstand. And wouldn't you know it, this Revelations chapter is not one of the short ones. There's a lot here to skim. I feel like I am back in Sunday school and I am being put on the spot. *Please God, help me find this.* I say that over and over in my mind. Jewel must think I'm an atheist and have never even opened this book before. Why do I get myself into situations like this? Jewel is the one who is supposed to be in the hot seat. Not me. Oh, wait a minute. Here's something. *Thank you, God!* I'm pretty sure I've found it. It is Revelations 12:7-9. To redeem myself, I will do my best to read this aloud and maybe even sound like a Lutheran minister. And so I begin:

> *The war broke out in heaven; Michael and his angels*
> *battled against the dragon. Although the dragon and*
> *his angels fought back, they were overpowered and lost*
> *their place in heaven. The huge dragon, the ancient*
> *serpent . . . was hurled down to earth and his minions*
> *with him. . . .*

I stop reading and look up to see if Jewel is impressed by my minister voice. But then I have to shake my head to let on that I do not quite understand what all this means.

"Ray, think about it: The so-called serpent and his angels are not cast into hell. Long, long ago, at the very beginning of time, they are hurled down to *earth,* not hell. The serpent then goes about his business. But thousands and thousands of angels—his minions—fall all over the earth. They land on mountains and hill-tops and in seas, lakes, and rivers. And they are not all bad angels. Some are compassionate and well-intentioned. They simply were in the wrong place at the wrong time. Not all were disobedient and rebellious. Nonetheless, they became the casualties of war. Like innocent civilians in any war, they got caught in the terrible cross-fire. And once they landed on earth, these refugees who had lost their eternal home, they had to make the best of the worst possible situation. Thus it all began.

"But Ray, you need to realize that's the biblical version of how all the *Huldre Folk* and other entities came to be. It was an explanation your Norwegian grandma could relate to. The so-called 'minions' have their own versions and their own origin stories about how they came to inhabit the earth. If one has an open mind, there is ample room for all the different stories and all the different versions."

Of everything that has happened today, I sure did not expect a Bible lesson from one of Lucifer's own. Maybe I did drown in the Red River this morning. And maybe this is my personal hell. *Uff da fida!*

But my new Bible teacher is not done yet. I can tell she has more she wants to tell me.

"Ray, the term that is used there in the Bible for the fallen angels is 'minions.' Does anyone ever stop to think about what that word means? The term 'minion' is related to the French word '*mignon*'—as in 'filet mignon.' In other words, the minions once were highly favored and highly desired. They were the 'choice' angels, the 'darlings' of heaven. But long ago, one celestial event changed their lives forever. They got caught up in something that just got bigger and bigger and soon spun out of control."

At last I nod in agreement. I kinda feel like I'm spinning out of control myself. And I suspect I've fallen into something that's a whole lot deeper than what I had expected. This stuff Jewel is telling me, it's an awful lot to take in and try to process.

You know, if you get stuck in the middle of a swamp and you're up to your neck in mud and muck, you can either keep trudging on or just head back. Either way, it's the same distance. Not sure where I learned that.

Lordy lordy, I suddenly realize it was my confounded curiosity that got me here. So I might as well see this through and keep muddying along. But I'm sure looking forward to setting foot on some solid ground again. For now, there are two words uppermost in my mind: "Land ahoy!"

CHAPTER 10

Yeah, my afternoon Bible lesson with Jewel Rhee, the fallen angel, is far from over. I don't believe all that she's telling me, but I do want to see where all this is going. Maybe I have missed my Grandma Knutson's stories more than I had realized.

"So am I seeing you the way you really are?" I ask Jewel. "Or are you a hideous creature with bat-like wings, cloven hooves, and a long tail?"

Truth be told, I am more confused and uncomfortable than I care to admit. So I try to sound like I am having a little fun. But Jewel isn't amused at all.

"Water spirits look different to different people. You see me as you want to see me. I'm able to change my shape accordingly. A Somali would see me the way a Somali has been taught to see me. Same for a Mandan, a Hmong, a Peruvian, a Sicilian, or an aboriginal Australian. This is why we go by so many different names. The Germans call us *Fenetten* or *Wassergeister,* the French *Dracae,* the Greeks *Naiads,* the Russians *Rusalky,* the Pawnee people *Tawakiks,* and so on. We are everywhere—in every lake, stream, and river. And because we are everywhere, stories are told about us all over the world. Now, could so many human storytellers in so many completely different cultures, be wrong?"

"But," I interject, "my grandma once told me that most of the *Huldre Folk* could not come to America because they were unable to cross water—and certainly not a big ocean. So most of them had to stay in Norway and Sweden and other parts of Europe. Guess they were landlocked."

"That may be, Ray. But water spirits have no problem crossing water or big oceans. Water is where we spend most of our time! If you listen closely to the stories told by the elders, you will understand all of this better. The elders' stories are not always entirely accurate, but they serve as a kind of basic guide for understanding the workings and wonders of the other world—a world that is largely unseen by the vast majority of humans."

"Maybe so," I counter, "but around here we seldom hear any of these old stories anymore. And even if we do, they're now considered children's fantasies or pure nonsense. No one talks about these things anymore. They would lock me up in a loony bin if I ever made a big deal about any of this. It's all a thing of the past. We just have to accept that."

Jewel nods in a sad kind of way and seems to share my assessment of the state of things.

"Yes, Ray, and what has all of this rational thinking and modernization brought you? Take a close look at the quality of the water in the rivers and streams today. Not far from here, there's a sewage plant. The smell of it can be sickening at times, and yet many families live nearby. People think nothing of dumping sewage or chemical waste into rivers that once were pristine and flowing free. It's hurting all of you and it's hurting all of us. This is what happens when people see a river as a thing or something that can be exploited. In this part of the country, rivers are our lifeblood. And so that is something all of us—humans and nonhumans—share in common. Water is life."

Ah, now I get it. This green-eyed woman is one of those environmental activists. She sure has opened up. And once she gets going, she sounds very passionate and even persuasive. Maybe I can ask something that will bring her back down to earth. Surely these Earth Day types will appreciate that.

"But if you are one of the ancient protectors of the rivers, why are things in such a sorry mess? Why aren't you doing more to protect the Red River and our other waterways?"

"We're trying, Ray. But we're experiencing a very serious crisis. The water temperature is getting warmer each year. Some of us are getting awfully weak and disoriented. And to complicate things, we are fighting among ourselves on a scale that we have not seen before. In some parts of the river, there is a vicious war going on between the 'Swanshees' and the 'Yuuzas.' These are nicknames we use to distinguish two of the more powerful groups in this section of the river. I belong to the Swanshees and we are the river's protectors. We try to keep the river clean and we try to promote some semblance of harmony. When humans or animals fall into the river, we try to rescue them. They seldom know it's us who are helping. We give them a gentle nudge and soon they find themselves on shore."

"Like me this morning?"

"Yes, Ray, like you. But with all those rocks, it required more than just a gentle nudge! Usually, we're invisible to humans and animals. But our presence can be felt or sensed. That is probably what has given rise to so many stories about us."

"If you are usually invisible, then why did I see you when you rescued me this morning? And why do I see you now?"

"Are you sure you see me now, Ray? What if you're talking to yourself? And what if all of this is just your imagination at work?"

I reach out and lightly touch Jewel's hands and face and hair.

"You certainly feel real," I admit. "And you look real. You're not invisible. Even that gal in the fast food place down in Wahpeton and all the people in the casino, they saw you. So now, what am I

73

missing here?"

"I'll let you in on a little secret, Ray. Here in this stretch of the Red River, the *Swanshees* came up with our own reward system for those who make a real effort to rescue humans. Any *Swanshee* who saves a human being from drowning can have a special day of their own. On that day, a *Swanshee* can assume human form and then get a close look at the human world. Because I saved you early this morning, I am enjoying my 'visible time' today. And thanks to your kindness, this day has been rather pleasant. I don't usually get to try new food or ride in a car or be inside a real casino."

"Okay," I say, scratching my head, "you've told me about the *Swanshees*. I think I get it. You're the good guys. But what about that other group you mentioned, the *Youhoozees?*"

"No, they are the *Yuuzas,* and the main thing you need to know about them is that they're predators. They do not save humans or animals. They lure them into deep water and they drown them. We call their leader 'Yangorr.' We suspect he's the one stirring up trouble in this portion of the river. He's what you humans might call a deviant—a psycho. Sometimes, the *Yuuzas* reach out and pull a deer or a human into the river. That kind of ultra-aggressive behavior wasn't tolerated in the past, but Yangorr has changed all that—at least for the time being. Humans and animals are not their only targets. If a *Swanshee* should grow weak or is not being watchful, it'll prove catastrophic. Ours has become a very dangerous world. Nowadays, when you or any human being enters the river, you risk your life."

All of this talk is giving me the shivers. And to think I was a sitting duck when I went into the Red River earlier today.

"Jewel, if the *Swanshees* are the protectors, then you need to do more to protect us humans. When we look out on the river, it looks so calm and peaceful. But now you are saying there's great danger only inches under the water. You and your group need to do more in your role as protectors."

"But Ray, we can't be everywhere at once. Yet we do what we can. Sometimes we are successful and at other times not. No matter how hard we try, we can't save everyone. Even the so-called 'good angels'—the guardian angels—they can't save all of the people they protect. Even though every human being is supposed to have his or her own guardian angel, thousands of people are killed every day. If the 'good angels' do not always succeed, how do you expect us to do so?"

"You're painting a pretty bleak picture," I say. "Can anything be done to thwart this Yangorr or to maximize your efforts? Anything at all?"

Jewel looks down at the three-strand gold ring on her finger to double-check that it is still there.

"With your help, Ray, I do have something in mind. That's why I asked you to take me down to Wahpeton today. I prevailed upon my friend Crystal to loan me this ring. It's supposed to be very powerful and maybe it will help the *Swanshees* in this portion of the river. At least it's worth a try, don't you think?"

"What makes the ring so special?" I ask. "Does it have supernatural power?"

"To be honest, Ray, I'm not quite sure. Crystal and I didn't have much time to talk. We spent most of our time arguing. She's very protective of the ring. All I know is that the area down by Wahpeton is very unique. They call it a vortex. It is where two rivers, the Bois de Sioux and the Ottertail, come together to form the Red River of the North. Each of the strands on this ring represents one of the three different rivers. According to our *Swanshee* legends, the ring was forged by an old blacksmith during a lightning storm long, long ago. I just hope the ring works and it will help us."

"So then," I wonder aloud, "are most of the *Swanshees* confined to the Red River area between Fargo and Wahpeton?"

"No," Jewel replies. "There are various *Swanshee* groups who range from Fargo to the Grand Forks area, and then up to

Winnipeg, and even all the way north to Lake Winnipeg in Canada. But remember, I'm simply using your names for the various cities and places on the river. We have our own ancient names and designations, which predate those to be found on any maps made by humans.

"You see, we have a long memory. Many of the present rivers actually are the remnants of ancient lakes. For example, the place where we are right now, it was the bottom of Lake Agassiz—one of the largest lakes in the entire world. But, as you can see, even enormous lakes can dry up or morph. Times change and conditions change. The one certain thing we *Swanshees* have learned is that everything changes. Nothing is permanent. And so we *Swanshees,* we change accordingly.

"Another thing," Jewel continues, "and I have said this before, the word '*Swanshee*' is just a nickname that we use for ourselves. We don't want others to know our real name. So I cannot reveal it to anyone. The name is very old and very sacred."

"Does the same go for that other group?" I ask.

"The *Yuuzas*? Yes, that's just a nickname, too. Their real name is too horrible to speak or even contemplate. I wish I could demonstrate, but I dare not. I do hope you'll keep your distance from Yangorr and the other *Yuuzas*. Otherwise, it would go very badly for you. And I would hate to see that happen.

"Ray, do you know what a *caribe* is—a South American piranha? Just imagine a hungry piranha with razor-sharp teeth that is the size of a human. That'll give you an idea of what you would be up against if you tangle with the likes of Yangorr. He'll wrap around you for a few torturous moments. And then he'll look into your eyes before going in for the kill."

"Are we still playing a game?" I innocently ask. "It's all starting to sound pretty bizarre and yet awfully serious."

"You'll need to decide for yourself," Jewel responds.

"But there are still things I don't fully understand. And forgive me, there are a lot of loose ends that I can't connect. For example, what about all those epitaph-songs that you sing? How do they fit in?"

"I already told you, Ray. On the days that I am visible and I am able to walk among humans, I sometimes go to the library. But I also like the peace and quiet of cemeteries. They are like libraries as well. And each gravestone is like a book with its own story. I read the names and the dates and I make up songs. It's just a quirk of mine. I find humans and human life fascinating. Endlessly fascinating."

"But what do you do about money—in case you need to buy something for yourself?"

Jewel laughs and actually slaps her knee.

"Money is so overrated! I rarely need money to buy anything at all. But if I did, I do have a stash of old coins, jewelry, and some really unusual meteorites. I know I could trade them for some modern currency. But I haven't had to do much of that."

"But surely you need money to buy food when you're mingling with humans. Don't you?"

"Well, have you seen me spend any of my own money today? Besides, people waste so much perfectly good food. It's never hard to find something to eat, even in a trash can. Sometimes, people will see me walking along the road and just offer me food. And going to a park after a big family picnic almost always results in an equally big paper plate full of angel food cake, colored marshmallows, potato salad, and pieces of watermelon. Some humans can be very generous."

"What's with the preference for black bananas and other soft food?"

"Ray, you're forgetting that I'm a *Swanshee*. We don't eat raw flesh or even any cooked meat. Our teeth aren't made for that. Now the *Yuuzas*, well, that's a different story. Someone like Yangorr can rip you to shreds in seconds!"

This young woman has an answer for everything. Either she might be telling me the truth, or she is one of the greatest liars known to humans, nonhumans, and all other life forms.

"You know, Ray, when people hear about spirits that dwell in the nearby lakes or rivers, they tend to discount the existence of such beings. And they do so readily. If people can't see supernatural creatures, they conclude that these creatures don't exist. But the irony is that water spirits are just as real as the water bears who coexist with us in our riverine environment."

Did she say "water bears"? Who is this strange woman trying to kid? For many years, I have walked along the Red River and not once (thank God) did I see a single bear—big or little. I look at Jewel and really roll my eyes to show her that this time, she's gone too far. I am not that gullible or naïve!

"Actually," Jewel calmly and matter-of-factly states, "some of your better scientists already know about the existence of water bears. These tiny animals also go by the name of 'tardigrades.' But the scientists have yet to realize how the water bears can teach humans how to survive. It's a real pity that most people can't see the water bears. They are really cute and they do look like tiny bears. But don't let that image fool you. They have three rows of teeth and the water bears are incredibly tough. During a prolonged drought, the water bears can live for years and years without any food or water. And no matter how hot or cold it gets, they quickly adapt. In many ways, they are indestructible. And they've been around for hundreds of millions of years.

"Yes, water bears are as real as the mosses and lichens in which they make their homes. If only given the opportunity, they can teach you so much. But they can't do that if your eyes are closed to their world and to all the other worlds that are within easy reach. The key to real wisdom is not knowledge. It's an open mind."

Well, this young woman is mighty clever and persuasive. And she knows how to put me on the spot. If I continue to argue with her, it will look like I am being terribly narrow-minded. So I think it's time to put the ball back in her court.

"Jewel, I'm still having some doubts. So how about a sign? Could you show me a sign? Something that only a *Swanshee* could do? That will make it easier for me to believe you."

"Not sure what kind of sign you're expecting. But tell you what, I do need to get up and use the bathroom."

"That's not really what I had in mind. Sounds like you're quite human, after all!"

Jewel laughs and I scoot back so that she has ample room to get up from the couch.

Come to think of it, this young woman goes to the bathroom a lot. I doubt if Jewel wears makeup, so I don't think she needs to powder her nose or reapply any lipstick. When she comes out of the bathroom, her face and the front of her blouse often are wet. And she doesn't even bother to dry herself off with a towel.

I figure the real reason Jewel goes to the bathroom so much is simply to splash some water on her face. Maybe she is indeed some kind of water creature and so she needs to freshen up now and then. I would like to ask Jewel about it, but it's just not proper to ask a woman what she does in the bathroom. Tillie certainly wouldn't have liked it. That I know for sure.

As Jewel heads toward the bathroom, she suddenly spins around and asks a question.

"You and Tillie had separate bedrooms, didn't you?"

I am so dumbfounded that I am unable to answer.

"The reason I ask," Jewel continues, "is that when you changed clothes earlier today, you got your things out of the one bedroom. But when you gave me some of Tillie's clothes, you took them out of a different bedroom across the hall."

"Yes," I admit. "I've got a pretty bad snoring problem, so some nights we did sleep in different bedrooms. That way Tillie could get a few hours of real rest and maybe even sleep through the night. And when she got so awful sick, well, she just stayed in that east bedroom. In case you must know, that is also the bedroom in which Tillie died."

Jewel looks at me as if she already knows all that I am telling her.

"After I'm done in the bathroom," Jewel adds, "I'd like to look around in Tillie's room. Would it be alright if I do that?"

Time and time again, I am surprised by the boldness of this young woman. It seems she will say whatever she pleases. Kind of reminds me of my Tillie.

And so I point to the east bedroom and I mutter a barely audible "yes."

CHAPTER 11

When Jewel goes into the bathroom, I sit on the couch in exactly the same place that she sat. I am not sure why I want to do this, but I do. I can feel the heat of Jewel's body on the couch cushions. I close my eyes, and only then do I realize how incredibly tired I am. It has been quite a day.

A few minutes later, I awaken and hear humming in the east bedroom. I call out "Jewel, Jewel," but she does not answer. I get up and go into the bedroom. And believe you me, I nearly faint from shock.

Tillie stands before me. She is dressed in a smart black and white outfit, and she wears her favorite red dress shoes.

"Who is Jewel?" Tillie asks. "You fell asleep on the couch and you were calling out the name 'Jewel.' Raymond, are you having an affair? Are you seeing another woman? Well, good grief, say something, Raymond. You act like you've seen a ghost."

I cannot move and I cannot speak. It's Tillie alright. And she's as talkative and peppery as ever. Sometimes, I cannot get in a single word.

"Wherever did you get those clothes, Raymond? They're so wrinkled. Looks like you've been laying around all day. Honey, are you alright? It's not polite to stare at people. You know how I hate that."

Tillie is right. She was raised on an Indian reservation, and she learned at an early age not to stare directly at someone. But at this moment I cannot take my eyes off her.

"How about we go dancing tonight, Raymond? I'm in the mood to kick up my heels and dance the night away. What do you say, honey? Shall we paint the town red—just the two of us?"

Oh Tillie, whatever did you see in me? We were so different. You loved to sing and dance and party. I had almost forgotten how full of energy you were and how you could bring even the stuffiest room to life.

"Tell you what, Raymond. You do look tired. We'll just stay home tonight. Okay? But I'm going to put some nice music on and we're going to dance in the living room. So head on out there. You're not going to stand me up tonight. No sir-eee. I need to shake a leg. And the exercise will be good for you."

Soon the music starts and we hear the sultry voice of Peggy Lee. My Tillie stands before me and we begin to dance. Peggy Lee sings of trains, soldiers, cowboys, and bluebirds. But it is hard for me to listen to all the words. I just stare into Tillie's dark eyes and I am lost in them. I hate dancing. But when I hold Tillie in my arms, the whole world falls away. And it is just the two of us dancing. Our feet move in time with the music, back and forth, back and forth. I deeply inhale her perfume and the sweet scent of her hair. Oh, the wonderful feeling of Tillie in my arms again. There is nowhere else that I would rather be. If this be love, let the music never stop. If this be heaven, let it last forever. And if this be eternity, let it begin now.

Alas, Peggy Lee stops singing and Tillie looks at me. Her dark eyes are filled with concern and sadness.

"Raymond, you're not going to do what you did this morning, are you? Promise me you won't do that ever again. It's just not right, Raymond. Besides, there's no rush. I'm in a good place now, Raymond. It doesn't matter if you come to me in ten minutes or in ten decades. I've got all the time in the world to wait.

"And Raymond, as I told you a couple of times before, you bear the name of a great Spanish saint. He managed to do one of the most miraculous things of all. Instead of getting beheaded or burned at the stake before he was even thirty, Saint Raymond was real careful. He didn't go sticking his neck out or looking for trouble. He just stayed indoors and prayed a lot and he wrote books. Books! And you know, he lived to be a hundred years old. For a saint to get to be that old back in those times, now that was a real miracle. So you take heed. And you take care of yourself, Raymond. You hear me?"

"Tillie," I say. Finally, I'm able to speak. Yet I fear that mere words might break the spell. But speak I must.

"Tillie, remember when we were here in the living room watching that last presidential debate? You were all for the female candidate and you said it was high time this country had a woman in charge. But I liked that other guy. I said he wasn't perfect, but at least he would be good for the small business folks. And he would win for sure. You got so mad at me and you called me a 'dumb Viking loser.' And then I called you a 'dumb Rooshun from the Rez.' I don't know what got into me when I said that. Walt had said something like that when he and I were arguing. And then those same words came out of my mouth. When you heard me utter those words, you seemed so hurt. We didn't sleep together after that for such a long time. But you and me, we never talked about it. Seems we kept waiting for the right time, but it just never came. Well, Tillie, I want to say it now. I'm so awfully sorry. Please forgive me, my dearest Tillie. Please."

"Yes, Raymond, I remember. I just couldn't understand why you would say a thing like that. I asked myself: Is that how my Raymond has seen me all these years—that I'm just a 'dumb

Rooshun from the Rez'? You know that 'Rooshun' is about the worst possible thing you can say to a German-Russian. It's like saying the n-word to an African-American. My daddy once punched a guy in the nose when that drunken fool hurled the word 'Rooshun' at him. Besides, as I told you many times before, my people came from the Odessa area. And that's in Ukraine, not Russia!"

"But Tillie, you did call me a 'dumb Viking loser.' So you're the one that brought nationality into it. I was pretty surprised, too."

"Oh Raymond, I called you a 'dumb Viking loser' because you were always cheering for the Minnesota Vikings and then getting so disappointed when they lost. You would get depressed for days after they lost a game."

"So you weren't calling me a dumb Norwegian loser? That's what I thought you meant!"

"Raymond, you know me. I don't mince words. If I had wanted to say that, I would have. But that is not what I said. I worried that the election would not go your way and then you would get all depressed again like you did every time the Vikings lost. So Raymond, don't worry about it anymore. It was just a misunderstanding. And you didn't know any better!"

We both laugh and then hug each other tightly. It's just like Tillie to be graceful and yet get the last word in to settle things.

Tillie pushes me over to the couch and makes me sit down beside her. She holds my hand as she speaks to me.

"Do you know one of the many things I love about you, Raymond Knutson? You are so unlike your brother Walt. I've told you before he's usually got his head up where the sun don't shine. But not you, Raymond. Your head is screwed on right. It really is. And it's tilted toward the stars. So if ever you get a little lonely or depressed, just go outside and look at all those stars. You may not always see them, but those stars are always there—just like me. So keep your head tilted toward the stars, Raymond. You do that and you'll always be alright.

"Now," Tillie says, "let's kiss and make up. It seems we haven't done that for ages and ages."

I do not argue. I close my eyes and I kiss my Tillie. As always, the sensation is warm and simply wonderful. We kiss for a long time. But I am an old man, and I do need to come up for air.

Tillie presses her lips on mine and she seems intent on sucking the very life out of me. I can hardly stand the pressure. Something isn't quite right here. Something is very, very wrong.

Uff da fida!

CHAPTER 12

I awaken to the sound of Peggy Lee singing the snappy tune "Fever." For a moment, I think I am in the old Powers Hotel in Fargo and listening to her perform on stage. I had always fantasized about that—to have actually been there. But Peggy Lee performed in Fargo way back in the 1930s. And that was well before my time.

My mouth hurts, and when I rub my lip I can see traces of red lipstick on my fingers. And then I remember what happened. Tillie!

Although I feel incredibly weak, I pull myself up from the couch and I search every room of the house. In the east bedroom, I see Tillie's black and white outfit hanging in the closet. And I smell her perfume. But Tillie is nowhere to be found.

Nor can I find any trace of Jewel. How strange! I interrupt Peggy Lee's singing and turn off the stereo. I go into the bathroom and wipe off the lipstick. Then I wash my hands and throw cold water in my face. After I dry myself off, I look in the bathroom mirror. The face that stares back at me is no movie star. I look like a sick old man.

The doctor told me that my terminal illness would cause me many problems—as would some of the strong medications I have to take daily. Maybe hallucinations and vivid dreams and wanting to wear women's lipstick are among the possible side effects?

Last Friday, on the day after my diagnosis, I sat in on a "convergent-imagery" therapy session at the hospital. The young woman doing the session had a crew cut and she sounded like a drill sergeant. She addressed us as if we were soldiers about to engage in battle. Those of us with malignant tumors were supposed to close our eyes and picture our tumors as evil monsters who had invaded our inner space. Then we were told to imagine that we had a defender, a warrior-type of the opposite sex, one who could fight the monster and overcome it. Guess it was some new "mind over matter" technique. So did I just imagine Yangorr of the *Yuuzas* as my personal monster, and Jewel Rhee of the *Swanshees* as my relentless defender? If so, I sure went overboard, and that means I am losing my grip on reality. It's one thing to imagine weird stuff, but it's a totally different thing to think it's all real.

I reflect on everything that has happened today. This is what I had worried about before ending it all. I don't want to become a basket case. Walt would sure get a good laugh if he saw me helpless and babbling to myself. I prefer to exit quietly and leave this earth with at least some dignity intact.

In the kitchen, I look out the back patio doors and I can see that it is getting dark. There is no movement down by the river. People who jog or take their dogs for a walk always try to be off the river by nightfall. But not me. There is some unfinished business. And this day, crazy as it has been, isn't over yet.

Again, I bring out the envelope that I had placed on the kitchen table earlier this morning. In big letters, I had printed on the outside of the sealed envelope: TO WHOM IT MAY CONCERN. Inside are my instructions for what to do with the funds in my checking and savings accounts, as well as the money from selling my house, car, and other belongings. One-third is to go to my Lutheran church here in Fargo; another third to Tillie's tipi-shaped Catholic church in Fort Yates; and the final one-third to that children's hospital back east. I trust my hurriedly-written will is official. I had my old banker friend Sig Dahlstrom notarize the one-page document a couple of days ago. He didn't even attempt to read it. Then again, I did keep talking to him while he notarized the document. Since I was a longtime customer, he didn't charge me a dime for the notarization. And he sent me off with a couple of still-warm sugar cookies. Banks will do anything these days to keep their customers happy, even become part-time bakeries.

As I look around the house, I take it all in and I smile to myself. Tillie and me, we didn't do so bad. Not bad at all. We had a lot of good years together. And then I remember something—Tillie's photo album of all the kids we helped at that children's hospital. I dust the album off and I actually kiss the front of the book. I do it the way those Catholic priests do when they're up on the altar saying Mass. I often wondered why they would kiss a book. Now I have a pretty good idea.

In an almost reverent way, I carry the big photo album into the kitchen and place it beside the "TO WHOM IT MAY CONCERN" envelope. Maybe the folks at the mortuary will display the album at the memorial service, the same way they did for Tillie. I am too worn out to write a special message and provide detailed instructions.

I put on a warm jacket and I empty out all the pockets. I look down at my shoes but decide not to change them. Then I close the door behind me and I walk all around the house as if I am inspecting the foundation. It feels good to walk around your house and not think about all the raking and winterizing that will need to be done. I am just going to let it all go this year.

As I head downhill toward the river, the crickets grow quiet. The river always looks different as it gets dark, especially in the fall. The trees and the bushes and even the grass seem to fade in and out. Or is it me? I may be really losing it.

At the river's edge, I pause and look at the slow-moving brown water. Red River! However did they come up with that name? In all my seventy years, I have never seen this river even slightly red. Brown. Brown is its color. And let's face it; on a night like this one, the color is a kind of crappy brown.

Just to double-check if they might be there, I want to call out the names of Tillie and Jewel. Not at the same time, of course. But at separate times. Oh, I have to restrain myself. I am not that far gone yet. No, not yet. But complete craziness probably will creep up on me before I know it.

A piece of gray driftwood floats by, heading downstream, heading north. That's another odd thing about this river. Most of America's rivers run south toward the sea. But not this one. Oh, no. The Red River heads in a completely different direction. This river runs north!

Something else is strange. Several of the rocks from this morning's mishap lay scattered around me. But I have no intention of picking up even one. Hey, wait a minute! Why are all these big rocks here and why are they scattered in roughly the same place where Jewel and I were this morning? Could all that stuff actually have happened?

No matter. A diseased brain can imagine anything and everything. I bend down to test the temperature of the river water, the same way I do when I check the bathwater before getting into the tub. The water in the river is extremely cold. It is October, after all.

As I gaze into the water, I see something. It almost looks like a face. Could it be Jewel? With my fingers, I splash around in the cold water. Maybe this is like knocking on someone's door. I have to make a splashing motion to announce my presence.

With the speed of lightning, something grabs my hand and pulls me into the cold depths of the river. I do not even have a chance to take a deep breath. The water rushes into my nose and mouth. Now, for the second time in one day, I feel like I am being water-boarded by a river! This must be some kind of record.

Oh my God! I feel something scaly and slimy wrapping around my face and torso and legs. Whatever it is, it's incredibly strong and it is pulling me down, down to the very bottom of the river. I open my eyes and I cannot see clearly, but this thing is ugly and it is turning me around like a top. I am getting dizzy. And with each turn, I feel my racing heartbeat slow and grow increasingly faint.

Now I open my mouth, and I say the words underwater, as bubbles of every size rise up all around me. I feel like I have lost gravity and I am somewhere up in outer space. The little bubbles look like multicolored stars and planets, and they are swirling around me at incredible speed. But somehow I manage to say the words underwater:

> *Nøkk, Nøkk, Nøkk!*
> *Calm the rivers,*
> *Calm the cricks.*
> *No more troubles,*
> *No more tricks.*
> *Nøkk, Nøkk, Nøkk!*

The thing that has entangled me immediately loosens its grip. But I am too cold and stunned and waterlogged to get away. And I am too weak to even care.

CHAPTER 13

Startling green eyes. Eyes I have looked into before. They are only inches away and they are peering into my own eyes.

I am on my back and I am wet and shivering. A young woman with startling green eyes and long red hair kneels over me. It is Jewel.

To my relief, when I reach down and touch my legs, I am still wearing my pants. Well, at least that little detail has changed. Thank my lucky stars!

Jewel breathes on my face and neck and she gently massages my arms and legs. Her hands are so incredibly warm.

"We have to stop meeting like this," Jewel jokes. Despite the trauma of the last few minutes, I have to laugh. And I spit out a mouthful of dirty river water when I do so.

"I wasn't trying to kill myself," I explain between gasps of air. "Something reached up out of the water and pulled me into the river. Was it you?"

Jewel frowns and looks into my eyes to indicate her disappointment that I would even think such a thing.

"You just had a near-death encounter with Yangorr of the *Yuuzas*," Jewel whispers. "But you and me, we showed him. He won't be bothering any of us ever again."

"How do you know? He's big and awfully strong, just like you said. And he's ugly as sin."

"Interesting choice of words," Jewel says. "But you did well, Raymond. You uttered that old *Nøkk* verse just in time. And you said it right. It countered his power immediately. When Yangorr let go of you and began to weaken, I moved in and jammed my three-strand ring right up against his—well, his body. And just to be sure, I gave him a farewell kiss."

"You did what?" I am absolutely disgusted. "You gave that ugly monster a kiss?"

"Uh-huh. And it really scared him. He wasn't expecting that at all."

"A kiss?" I still cannot believe it.

Jewel stops massaging my arms and legs. She looks at me for a long time. It is dark, but I can see her startling green eyes in the moonlight.

"Raymondo, I have a confession to make. This afternoon in your house, I changed shape and became Tillie for a few minutes. I wanted you to see her again and to dance with her. I know how much you miss her. You had asked me to give you some kind of sign. Remember? I thought bringing Tillie back to you for at least a few minutes would be the best and surest sign of all."

"But," I stammer, "how did you know the way her voice sounded and how she talked to me?"

"Oh Ray, I often watched you and Tillie when you walked along the river here. I saw both of you and heard both of you talk and swap stories. I was invisible then, so you never saw me. I'm sorry I eavesdropped so much, but I was fascinated by the two of you. Of all the couples who I have seen strolling along this river over the millennia, you two were among my all-time favorites. At times, you made me wish I were human. Ah, to know such love. You give the rest of us creatures hope."

"Speaking of hope," I respond, "I'm hoping you might remember that I'm a sick old man who is about to catch his death of cold for a second time today. We're both wet and shivering. We need to get inside and warm up. And we need to be quick about it."

"Tell you what," Jewel says. "There's something else I need to tell you. And it's very important. But right now, let's go up to your house and change into some dry clothes. And we need to wear some really nice clothes. We have a party to go to this evening. And we can't miss it."

"But I don't like parties," I protest. "Why do I have to go? Why can't I just go to bed? Will this day ever end?"

As we go up the hill, I start to hyperventilate. And so we stop for a short break. Jewel holds me close and patiently waits for me to start breathing normal again.

"Ray," the green-eyed Jewel says, "I think I have one of those Ole and Lena stories for you."

"You do? Oh, this is one I want to hear."

Jewel looks at me and actually seems a little nervous. But then she begins.

"You know, Ole and Lena were getting up there in years. But this one evening, Lena was in a romantic mood. So she took a long bath and she was in the bathroom for such a long time. Ole was sitting on the couch in the living room and watching the Minnesota Vikings on TV. The Vikings were losing again, so Ole was half-asleep. When Lena came out of the bathroom, she was wearing only her bathrobe. She sat on the couch right beside Ole and she hoisted up her bathrobe a little to show her legs.

"'*Vell denn, how do I schmell?*' Lena asked. Ole was still half-asleep, but he leaned over and sniffed the air and he said, '*Youu schmell goot. Yah, youu schmell preedi goot.*' Lena smiled and said, '*Toonight, I took me a milk bath. Yah, I fillt up da tubb vith varm milk und I took me a nice loong bath. In milk, Ole!*' He seemed very surprised. '*Grade A?*' asked Ole. '*Yah shure,*' Lena replied. '*I'de*

93

give it an A. Mabee even a A plus!' Now Ole wanted to know more. *'Homo-genized?'* he asked. *'Ach, no,'* Lena answered. *'It vas chuust straight milk. Yah, da milk vas straight.'* Ole wanted to know even more. *'Pasteurized?'* he asked. *'Oh, no,'* Lena said with a laugh. *'None of it vent past my eyes. Chuust up to my chin!'* And oh, how Lena laughed and laughed. *'Past youur eyes! Hah, dat's a goot one!'* said Lena to Ole. *'Yah, past youur eyes!'"*

I try hard to keep a straight face, but I can't. I laugh, not so much at the joke, but at the way Jewel tells it. She goes a little over the top with the mixed Norwegian and German accents, but that's what makes it even funnier.

Now I have to remind myself that Jewel never laughed at any of my Ole and Lena jokes. So I am thinking about what to say.

"Well," Jewel asks. "Was it okay? Did I tell it right?"

"Naahh," I answer in a very disapproving tone of voice. "And since you're not a real Norwegian, I may have to report you—to NAAHH."

"What is NAAHH?" Jewel asks with a look of real concern.

"You don't know what that is? It's the Norwegian-American Anti-Harassment Headquarters—NAAHH for short. Yeah. And it's based right here in Fargo."

"Really?"

"Naahh," I reply. And I wrinkle my nose and try to sound like a lost and disgruntled goat as I say it. *"Naahh! Naahh! Naahh!"*

CHAPTER 14

Despite Jewel's urgings, I refuse to wear a suit jacket and tie. Instead, I put on a nice button-down shirt and some casual slacks. And I also wear an insulated jacket with a hood. I am not taking any chances with this October weather.

When Jewel comes out of Tillie's room, I have to smile. Like Tillie, this young woman knows how to dress. She has her hair up and she wears a pink blouse, black slacks, and red zip-up boots. To top it all off, she adds a brightly-colored plaid jacket. It is the kind you see out in Bismarck and the western part of the state, but only rarely in Fargo.

"Dressing up is fun," Jewel declares. "Especially when you're going to a party. Are you ready, Raymondo Knutson of Fargo?"

"I guess I'm as ready as I'll ever be, Jewel Rhee of the *Swanshees.*"

The kitchen clock indicates it is well after eight o'clock. Usually by this time of the day, I am feeling pretty pooped and I often fall into bed. Before I got so sick, I could at least make it to 10:30 in the evening. That way I could watch the news, weather, and sports reports. But this young green-eyed woman won't let me rest. And now we have to go to a party somewhere. A party! I don't even know what kind it is and Jewel won't tell me much.

"What time does this event start?" I ask.

"Don't worry. It'll begin when we get there. So just relax a bit."

"I do hope it's just a small gathering. I hate crowds. And now I gotta find my car keys."

"No need," Jewel tells me. "We can walk there. It's not far."

"Oh God," I moan again. "Don't tell me we're going over to Mrs. Gunderson's down the street. She's always trying to get me over there for a Christmas party or a *Syttende Mai* brunch. I'm running out of excuses why I can't attend."

"That's not where we're going, Ray. But before we go, we do need to talk. Or rather I need to talk and you need to listen. It's very important."

"A matter of life and death?" I joke.

"Yes," says Jewel, "yes, it is. So maybe you better sit down."

We both take off our coats and I go over to the living room couch. But as I sit down, the words "life and death" seem to have triggered something.

"What's wrong?" Jewel asks. "Don't you want to hear what I have to tell you?"

"No, it's not that," I murmur. "I just remembered something Grandma Knutson told me when I was a boy. It was a riddle, and I'm pretty sure it was about a boy who hurt himself on the Red River. The way she told it, I think it was her own subtle way of endorsing my future attempt at suicide."

"Oh, Ray, are you sure? Why would a grandmother tell a young grandson something like that? It doesn't sound possible. How does your grandmother's riddle go?"

"Unfortunately, I don't quite remember. But it was about a boy who intentionally hurt himself. It began with words like 'the living and the dead, on the River Red, they are offering you a riddle, so you must use your head.' But I can't remember how the rest goes. It's kinda long and involved. I only know bits and pieces. But now that I'm thinking and talking about it, I'm getting this really strange feeling."

"Ray, do you have anything that belonged to your Grandmother Knutson? Maybe something that she actually wore or really treasured?"

I know just the thing. So I point to the east bedroom.

"Go in Tillie's room there and you'll see a big tall dresser. On the top of that dresser is an old jewelry box that is decorated with painted flowers and the Norwegian phrase 'Se, men ikke rør.' I'm guessing it means something like 'Look much, but don't touch.' Jewel, you can go ahead and open that box. Inside, you'll see a heart-shaped brooch with little silver and gold spoons hanging from it. That piece was Grandma's pride and joy. It was a wedding gift that had been given to her own grandmother back in Norway. So it's old—very old."

Jewel soon appears and hands me the family heirloom. She is very careful and treats the object delicately. I look down at the brooch and feel its weight in the palm of my right hand. From the lower portion of the heart hang nine tiny silver and gold spoons. Despite their age, the dangling spoons still have a shimmer about them.

"Ray, just sit back and hold that brooch tight. Close your eyes and picture your Grandma Knutson the way she looked when she told you all those stories and riddles. If all goes well, you're going to see her again and you can ask her about that old riddle. Okay? So relax. And think about her, think about her, think. . . ."

In no time at all, I am in Grandma Alma Knutson's old farmhouse. My parents and Walt and me, we lived with her for a few months after our house burned down. Every night at bedtime, Grandma would come into the room where I slept. She would tell me stories about the *Huldre Folk*. Sometimes, she would recite poems and humorous rhymes. And there would always be a difficult riddle or two to solve.

"Grandma," I begin, "no matter how hard I try, I just can't get that one riddle you told me—the one about the boy and the River Red. How does it go, Grandma? Do you remember?"

The old woman's eyes come to life and she sits straight up on the edge of the bed. She looks at me and says the piece with a sing-song cadence that is truly magical. She sounds like a Norwegian-American rap artist, and she even moves her head and body in time with all the words:

The living and dead
on the River Red
offer you this riddle
so use your head.

One day, one day,
on the River Red
a boy fell down
and lost his head.

And on that day
on the River Red
the boy got up
and found his head.

And on that day
on the River Red
the boy he stared
at his empty head.

And on that day
on the River Red
the boy set fire
to his empty head.

The living and dead
on the River Red
offer you this riddle
so use your head.

Yes, that's it; that sounds like the riddle. But is that all there is? I had remembered it being even longer and more complicated. No matter, I have heard enough to know that this strange riddle predicted my own attempt to end my life. Grandma must have sensed that one day I would be a danger to myself.

"I'm sorry, Grandma, but only now do I realize I am that boy in your riddle. You were warning me. Weren't you? I am the boy on the River Red who lost his head for a moment and then tried to self-destruct. So that's it then. I have solved the riddle. Right?"

Grandma Knutson laughs and shakes her head. She even slaps her hands together and then lightly slaps the sides of her face. She is thoroughly enjoying the moment. Evidently this grandmother really had it out for me.

"Oh, Raymond," she exclaims, still laughing. "You are so wrong! But there is a lesson here. Sometimes, when a person hears something really strange, a person is thrown by the strangeness of it all. And because of that, they don't get its real meaning. That is the power of the riddle. And that is the power of words.

"The boy in that riddle," the old woman continues, "isn't you, Raymond. No sir! It was my husband Oskar—your Grandpa Knutson. And it all really happened to him, and so he composed that riddle. And then I kept that riddle going long after he left us."

"What do you mean, Grandma, that the boy in the riddle was Grandpa? Did he really set fire to himself?"

Again, the old woman laughs so hard that the bed and the quilts and all the pillows shake. She is having quite a time. And it takes her a while to regain her composure.

"Lordy lordy, the things you come up with, Raymond! But don't you feel bad. When I first heard that riddle, I couldn't solve it either. And I got kinda mad at Oskar. A lot of people who heard that riddle couldn't figure it out. Yah, it stumped even our older, educated folks.

"Well, here's how Grandpa would explain it—after everyone who had heard it just gave up and begged for the answer. When Oskar was a boy growing up on a farm north of Fargo, he went over to a friend's house to carve pumpkins one night. You see, it was Halloween time. On the way home, he took the old river trail. But it was getting dark and he got real scared. He started running and he tripped and fell. And that big carved pumpkin went a rolling. But little Oskar, he got up and found the pumpkin and then he just kept on running till he got home. That night, he stared at that big ol' jack-o'-lantern. And he put a candle inside. Then he took out a match and lit it. And that carved pumpkin lit up the whole room.

"So you see, Grandpa was telling the truth in that riddle of his. He surely was. It all actually happened to him. So it was all true, all true."

I am amazed by the simplicity and innocence of it all. Grandma has a way of explaining things and making anything and everything seem obvious and believable.

"But why," I ask, "does the riddle start out and end the way that it does, with those words about 'the living and the dead offering you this riddle'? That really threw me. So I'm still not sure about that part."

"Oh Raymond, that riddle is offered by both the living and the dead. Oskar and many others who knew that riddle are gone now. Don't you see? But if people like you remember that riddle and pass it on, then it is a gift. Yah, it's an offering from the dead to the living. And a thing like that, simple as it is, connects all of us—the living and the dead—through all the years and all the generations.

But you gotta remember the old words and ways and pass them on. Or they're lost forever."

Grandma Alma Knutson now does something that I remember her doing at the close of many of her bedtime storytelling sessions. She cups her freckled and wrinkled hands together and gently blows on them. Then she extends her cupped hands to me and says: "See, it's still there. It's not a very big flame, but it's still burning. Here, Raymond, I pass the fire on to you. Can you feel it? Can you sense its power? Take this fire and keep it burning. Will you do that, Raymond? Will you?"

When I open my eyes, Grandma Knutson is gone and I am back on the living room couch. Jewel sits beside me and she is smiling.

"Did you see your grandmother, Ray? And did you get a chance to ask her about the riddle?"

"Yes," I reply. "I saw her and I spoke to her. And I got some answers. It was amazing. She looked just like she did when I was a kid. Grandma's eyes really lit up when we talked."

"She sure wasn't that way when she left us years ago. On the day grandma died, she seemed delirious and was saying the same thing over and over again. The minister was at her side and he said she kept repeating the phrase 'they walk amongst us' in Norwegian. The minister assumed she must have been talking about the angels. But I often wondered if she wasn't referring to the *Huldre Folk* instead. After all, the 'Unseen Ones' were as real to her as her own children and grandchildren.

"I really miss the Grandma Knutson of my younger years. So this little visit back in time was quite a treat for me. Grandma always had a way of lifting my spirits. And she did it again today—all these many years later."

Yet my visit with Grandma Knutson never would have been possible without Jewel. I still haven't figured out this green-eyed woman to my complete satisfaction. But I do know Jewel is a real wonder worker of sorts. And I also know there is something I have to do.

"Jewel," I say, "I want you to have this old brooch. And I know Tillie and Grandma Knutson would want you to have it, too. Here, let me pin it on you to see how it looks."

True to her name, Jewel Rhee does not refuse the gift. Her startling green eyes and radiant smile tell me she is appreciative and even touched.

Now I lean forward a bit and I just stare at Jewel. She seems puzzled by the intense way I am studying her from head to toe. I look at her forehead to see if I can detect any beads of sweat. I check her facial color and I even look down at her hands to see if they are shaking.

"Congratulations," I finally announce to Jewel. "You've passed my test. If you had been one of the bad *Huldre Folk,* this brooch would have weakened and sickened you. Back in Norway, these objects were not just pretty pieces of jewelry. They were worn at baptisms, weddings, and funerals. And their purpose was to protect the wearer and to ward off evil beings and evil spirits. So now you and I both know: You are truly one of the 'good' *Huldre Folk.*"

Tears fill the startling green eyes of Jewel. She rubs the brooch and seems to draw renewed energy from it each time she touches the object. For us Knutsons, it was a family heirloom. But for Jewel, the brooch is a badge of honor.

"Ray, I still have something important to tell you. Remember when Tillie kissed you so long and so hard this afternoon?"

"Yes, but that wasn't my Tillie. You told me it was you masquerading as Tillie. But you couldn't fool me. I knew it wasn't her. She never kissed me like that. Not even when we were younger. You were pretty rough. I felt like a vacuum cleaner was trying to pull out my insides. It knocked the wind out of me!"

"I had to do that, Ray. I'm sorry I kissed you so hard, but I had to suck that horrible thing out of you—that thing that was making you so sick and killing you. That's why, when I was in the river and fought Yangorr, I had to kiss him. And when I did, I spewed all of that horrible stuff into him. It's something we *Swanshees* can do. It's called 'justifiable transference' in our world. So now Yangorr has that disease and he has to deal with it."

"So that's it," I reply, and I can feel my blood pressure rise as well as my voice. "You used me as bait! Bait! It was all an elaborate plot today. The rescue this morning. The trip to Wahpeton. The ring from Crystal. The encounter with Yangorr. All an elaborate plot. I could have drowned. I could have been torn to pieces. I could have been killed!"

"Please, Ray," Jewel says, her green eyes glowing bright. "Spare me. Isn't killing yourself what you were intending to do anyway? So don't get all self-righteous with me, Ray. I know better. And you know better, too."

At the moment, I don't know what to think. I look down at my feet and I study my shoes.

"Ray, I think you're missing the real point here. You're no longer an ill person who is dying. Your medical condition is not 'terminal.' You've been cured."

It takes a while for the words to sink in. Could it be? Is this why I seem to have more pep tonight and why I haven't fallen asleep yet? It is way past my usual bedtime.

"So I don't have to take my meds anymore?"

"That's right. But I suggest you have your doctor check you over and see what he thinks. Just to be sure, of course."

"If I am cured, won't the doctor get suspicious that suddenly I'm a well man again? He'll ask lots of questions. What do I tell him—that a green-eyed water creature from the Red River kissed me and that's what cured me?"

"How open-minded is your doctor? Is he a Scandinavian like yourself?"

"No, I think he's an Indian—an Indian from India."

"Then go ahead and tell him. He'll understand. You know, the rivers and streams there in the Indian subcontinent are filled with water spirits. And they go by many different names. Better yet, say nothing to your doctor. Just let him scratch his head and wonder. It's good for doctors. Keeps them somewhat humble. They need that once in a while."

After Jewel and I put on our coats, we head out the front door. She directs me to go around to the back of the house. And she holds on to me as we head down to the river. It is awfully steep in places. But the moon is full, and so we have enough light to see where we're going.

CHAPTER 15

When we get to the river, there are more than a hundred individuals waiting. Some of them look very different and a few are wearing really bizarre masks. I do not know a single one of them. But they wave to us as we arrive and they all seem to know Jewel.

"We want to have a little celebration tonight!" Jewel shouts out. It appears she is the mistress of ceremonies and maybe the organizer of this event.

"Yes, there is real cause to celebrate!" Jewel continues to shout out. "Yangorr of the *Yuuzas* is no longer a threat to us. And the one we have to thank is Raymond Knutson. He's our long-time neighbor. And now he is our life-long friend!"

They are a quiet bunch. Instead of cheering or applauding, Jewel and all of those gathered raise both their arms and make a strange, pushing-up gesture, as if they are shooting free throws toward the moon. They keep this up for quite some time. The group is different alright and I am kinda fascinated. At least they're not too wild and rowdy. Mrs. Gunderson and my other neighbors will appreciate that.

I lean in towards Jewel and whisper, "Did all of the folks here save a life today? Is that why they're visible to me?"

Jewel smiles and whispers back that tonight is a special occasion, and there are exceptions. "We don't always follow the rules," she explains, "we've learned how to bend them now and then."

My *Swanshee* hostess now directs me to look straight ahead, toward the river flowing north. Tiny red particles fall like snowflakes all around us. Soon the river is bathed in a scarlet, iridescent light. I look up and down and cannot see where all of the red light is coming from. But the whole scene is beautiful. For once, this river looks like the "River Red."

Off to our right, on a grassy knoll, a group of Native American men sit around a large drum and raise their voices in song. A couple of the larger men sing such high notes that at times it sounds like falsetto. The men sing in unison and they beat the drum so hard that even the ground seems to quiver a bit. Four Indian women stand behind the men, and the women sing and move their bodies in time with the drumming. At times, the women make a trilling sound that makes the hair on the back of my neck stand on end.

"Of all the many human groups who have lived in this part of the country," Jewel softly explains to me, "none has been as respectful as the indigenous people. The song they are singing celebrates the earth, the sky, the water, and all the nations of this land—animal, plant, human, and nonhuman. That song is like a national anthem, and yet it recognizes no national boundaries or borders. The song includes everyone and all of creation. We *Swanshee* love it, and so we include it at many of our gatherings."

I nod my head because I have heard similar sentiments before, from my Tillie. She was a proud German-Russian, but she was just as proud of the Native American heritage that she was exposed to at such an early age back on the Standing Rock Reservation. Tillie felt right at home at powwows, rabbit dances, and Indian taco parties—just as she did at German-Russian Oktoberfests, polka dances, and *Blachenda*-eating contests. That Tillie, how I wish she could see all of this now. She would smile from ear to ear.

The singing and drumming suddenly stop and soon we see fire-works exploding in the river, well under the surface. It is as if the fireworks are being reflected in the river, but there are no fire-works above us. And they are as brilliant as they are silent. Because it is so quiet, one can easily hear all the "ooohs" and "ahhhs" of those gathered.

With a wave of the hand, Jewel asks us to look toward the left bank of the river. A red spotlight beams down from somewhere and we see a large wooden stage. About a dozen men and women take their places on the stage, including three fiddlers and a guitar-player who are seated close together.

"We now welcome some Métis musicians and dancers from the Turtle Mountain area of North Dakota," Jewel announces. "They are the descendants of the early French and British fur traders and voyageurs who intermarried with the Chippewa and Cree people. These folks are going to perform for us 'The Red River Jig.' Feel free to jig and move about as you hear this incredible ensemble. There is a lot of history in this music, and there is pain and joy and triumph. Take it away, Turtle Mountain musicians and danc-ers!"

The lead fiddler, an elderly man wearing a white cowboy hat and freshly-polished boots, nods and starts playing. His feet move rapidly and you can hear his boots on the wooden stage. All of the other musicians and dancers soon join in and the jigging gradually becomes louder and faster. Several of the dancers yell and shout, urging the musicians to increase the tempo. Everyone in the crowd now moves their feet in time with the music as well. The sound is infectious, and no one can resist the impulse to join in the non-stop jigging. For nearly ten minutes, the musicians play and they grin and laugh as they watch the reaction of the crowd. Sweat runs down the faces of the musicians and dancers. Finally, the lead fid-dler gives the signal and "The Red River Jig" comes to a thunder-ous end. By now everyone is in a state of near-euphoria. I can feel my heart beating hard and fast, but it is a mighty good feeling. We raise our arms and push and push. What a performance!

After the Métis musicians and dancers make their exit, a large group of children fills the stage. They appear to range in age from five to thirteen. A little girl wearing a large white bow in her hair comes forward. She stands on the edge of the stage and giggles as she steps into the gaze of the red spotlight. She can barely reach the microphone, and at times she stands on her tiptoes to do so.

"*Bonsoir*," the little girl sings out. "Good Evening, everybody! My name is Elisa and I'm from the St. Boniface area of Winnipeg, Canada. We are your neighbors to the north. Like you, we also live on *la Riviére Rouge*—the Red River. In St. Boniface, we speak both French and English. So I hope you can understand me! We're only a few of the many children who Raymond and Tillie have helped over the years. We want to say to them: *Merci mille fois plus*—Thank you a thousand times and more! And now, we have a French song that we want to sing for all of you. It is a song about a lovely fountain. The song is our way of saying to Raymond and Tillie that we will never, ever forget them or any of the other people who have been so kind and have helped us."

As Elisa and the children begin to sing, a large fountain bubbles up and springs out of the Red River. The fountain is enveloped in red light and the waters keep spiraling up and up, until they seem to bathe the very stars that shine above us so brightly. At times, the fountain changes from one bright color to another. And all the while, the children sing:

> *À la claire fontaine,*
> *M'en allant promener*
> *J'ai trouvé l'eau si belle*
> *Que je m'y suis baigné.*
> *Il y a longtemps que je t'aime,*
> *Jamais je ne t'oublierai....*

When the children finish, the enormous fountain slowly grows smaller and smaller until it disappears under the slow-moving waters of the Red River. Everyone in the crowd raises their arms and pushes back and forth. But I am so overcome with emotion that I barely can lift a finger. Each of the children who steps off the stage comes over to me and gives me a big hug. And I hear the words "thank you" in at least a half-dozen different languages. The last child to hug me is little Elisa, and she hugs me twice to let me know that Tillie is remembered, too.

The red spotlight slowly dims and there are a few minutes of near-darkness and silence. But it is not too dark to see that Jewel is looking at me and smiling in a strange kind of way. I try to compose myself and I ask if the show is over, or if there might be more to come. But she just smiles and smiles.

Now Jewel motions for me to look toward the stage as the red spotlight shines down once again. This time the red light is even more intense. A woman is standing on the stage and she is wearing a long white gown. She has her back to the crowd and she seems to be meditating or maybe taking a deep breath. When she turns around, she is snapping her fingers and singing. She has blond hair, long eyelashes, and a telltale beauty mark. I cannot believe my own eyes. It's Miss Peggy Lee!

Even though Peggy Lee has no microphone, her distinctive and haunting voice can be heard up and down the length of the river. But where's the orchestra? We can hear the brass and the other musicians, yet we cannot see them. Nonetheless, this is quite a show. Peggy Lee sings "I'm a Woman" and a couple of her other more popular songs. When she finishes each number, everyone shows their appreciation by raising both arms and rapidly doing the free-throw gesture. I find myself doing so as well. The night air is charged with such electricity and excitement. Wow! Peggy Lee is back in Fargo and performing on stage again.

The red light softens a bit and someone hands Miss Peggy Lee a microphone that resembles a sparkly magic wand. She looks into the crowd of faces and evidently feels compelled to say something about her next song.

"It feels great to be back in North Dakota, and to stand before such a warm and appreciative audience. No doubt about it! But there is some doubt and debate about this next number. The good folks down in Texas and Oklahoma, they claim it's a song about their part of the country. But we here in the Upper Midwest, well, we know better. Don't we? We've always believed this beautiful folksong is about a Métis girl who falls in love with a soldier who must go to war. And he has to leave that lovely girl behind. I'm pretty sure you all know the words, especially the chorus. And you know something else: *This is our song.* It's called 'The Red River Valley.'"

As Peggy Lee sings the familiar old tune, everyone softly joins in and we sway with the gentle and hypnotic music. I look at Jewel and she is smiling, but there are also tears in her eyes. Boy, does this old song have an effect on people. As I look around, I see other individuals dabbing at their eyes as well. Many of us reach out and we even hold hands, as if we are one big family. When Peggy Lee gets to the chorus, we join in. And as we sing, we look at the Red River that is flowing by so peacefully only a few steps away:

> *Come and sit by my side if you love me,*
> *Do not hasten to bid me adieu*
> *But remember the Red River Valley*
> *And the girl who has loved you so true.*

After Peggy Lee finishes the song, we all raise our arms and push up toward the moon. But we do so in a restrained and almost reverential manner. "The Red River Valley" is not only our song, it is a deep part of all of us. Every so often—like tonight—we are reminded just how deep down that old song goes.

As we were all singing along with Peggy Lee, I saw Jewel hurry off toward the back of the stage. Poor girl! Tonight she is in charge and she really has her hands full. But everything is going so smoothly and everyone is in such a joyful and upbeat mood.

"And now," a strange man in a colorful mask shouts out for all to hear, "we are pleased to introduce the wife of Raymond. Here she is, Tillie 'Red Foot' Knutson. She will dance to a special number by Miss Peggy Lee. Please take it away, Tillie!"

Oh, I can hardly believe it. There's my Tillie! She is on the same stage as Peggy Lee. Tillie is wearing red tap shoes and there's a bright red bow in her hair. And she does not miss a beat. She holds her own and still manages to wave at me now and then. Everyone is watching Tillie's feet and all of her fancy dance moves. She is most impressive. When Tillie finishes, all the spectators raise their arms high and they do the rapid free-throw gesture toward the moon. And no one pushes up toward the moon more than me. I am so proud of my Tillie.

Now Peggy Lee tells us she is going to perform the final number of the evening. And I am asked to come up on stage and dance with Tillie as Peggy Lee sings! I want to hide. I want to get out of here and fast. But I am also torn. While I certainly do not want to dance in front of these folks, I do want to hold Tillie again. So I slowly walk up to the stage and I feel a whole lot better when I embrace my Tillie. And then we start to dance. We sway and keep time to the music. But this song is longer than most of Peggy Lee's regular numbers. For some reason, it seems different, and I feel that she is singing to me.

The funny thing is that over the years, I have heard Peggy Lee's "Is That All There Is?" countless times. But tonight, the song suddenly sounds very personal. And I hug Tillie tight as I listen to the words. Peggy Lee is looking right at me as she talks and sings. In the song, she sings about things that never seemed connected in my own mind until now: a terrible house fire during childhood; a circus that comes to town; a lover who is suddenly gone; and the utter foolishness of contemplating an act of self-destruction. It is as if I am hearing this song for the very first time.

Oh, the song is powerful alright. It hits me so hard that Tillie has to help me stay upright. Maybe that is why Peggy Lee saved it for last. I kiss Tillie and hold her for a long time.

Suddenly, my Tillie and all the performers and the bright red lights and the wooden stage are gone. I keep opening and closing my eyes to bring it all back, but I am unable to recreate the scene as it was.

Now it is just Jewel Rhee and me standing on the banks of the river. We are both quiet for a long time.

"Wow," I finally say to Jewel. "This was the best party I've ever been to by far. And seeing Tillie dance and then holding her in my arms again. Oh, that topped it off. It was simply spectacular. Yes, that's the word. It was spectacular."

"I'm so pleased, Ray. We didn't have much time to prepare, but things fell into place. I have a good group here. They can do just about anything. Illusion, magic, and shape-shifting are our specialties. And we have eons of experience. All that comes in handy, you know."

"Jewel, you seemed to be in charge tonight. So is there something you haven't told me? Are you the head of all the *Swanshees*?"

"No, no. Not at all. I'm just a local organizer. The day I become the *Swanshee* Sovereign is, well, as unlikely as—"

"As unlikely as Walt and me becoming bosom buddies?" I respond with a slight laugh. "Yeah, there are things in this world that have about as much of a chance as a snowball in—in a red-hot forge. Right? But Jewel, you clearly have all the qualities of a great and fair-minded leader. You really do."

"Believe me, Ray, I'm fine just being a local organizer."

We both look up just as a shooting star sends a wispy trail across the overarching sky.

"Dearest Ray, I'm afraid the time has come. You need to return to your world and I need to go back to mine."

I do not like what I'm hearing and Jewel knows it. I kick and scratch at the ground with the tip of my right shoe, and I keep at it as she talks.

"Ray, I really appreciate that old brooch you gave me. I'll treasure it always. In return, I wanted to give you a similar kind of token as a reminder of the time we spent together today. But our *Swanshee* things are not very permanent in your world. I'm sure you know that old saying—'Here today, gone tomorrow'? It's hard to explain, but it's kind of like that."

"Sounds like the elusive gold of the leprechauns," I say. "So tell me, Jewel, am I really part Irish?"

"Oh, does it really matter?" Jewel quickly responds. "Irish. Norwegian. German-Russian. Métis. Somali. You are who and what you think you are. *You are you.*"

"Fair enough—then how about some parting *Swanshee* words of wisdom?" I ask. "Maybe you've got some answers as to how we humans should deal with the really big questions, the ones about life and death?"

Jewel's smile turns into a slight frown. She looks like a teacher who's just been asked to reveal the answers to a student preparing for a final exam.

"The answers you'll have to discover for yourself, Ray. You know that. Besides, it's more fun that way. But as an outsider, I can offer some friendly advice. When it comes to life: Respect it, cherish it, and celebrate it."

"Like we did tonight?"

"Yes, Ray. Like we did tonight. Humans spend way too much time working and worrying. And they spend too little time celebrating the sheer joy of being alive."

"That makes sense," I say. "And what about death?"

Jewel steps forward to look directly into my eyes. I take it she really wants me to get this and she isn't going to repeat it.

"My advice in dealing with death is fairly simple: Respect it, challenge it, and DELAY IT!"

"Is that advice just for me or the whole human race?" I meekly ask.

"Oh, I'm pretty sure you know who that advice is aimed at, Raymondo."

We both laugh and Jewel jokingly tugs at my pants leg—probably to remind me that earlier this morning, I stood before her without any pants.

"Do you think you can make it up to your house alright?" she asks.

"Ah," I say. "With that big moon overhead, I'll be fine. But Jewel, tell me, will I get to see you again?"

"I'm not sure, Raymondo. Eventually, I need to go back to Wahpeton and return this ring to Crystal. And you do have all those casino coupons. So one never knows. I can't make any promises. But every time you walk along the river here, you'll be seeing and touching a part of me. Remember that. And if you decide to organize a group to pick up some of the trash along the river once in a while, I'd appreciate it. If you could just fish out all those plastic bags and plastic straws, that would be a start. Whoever invented those awful things? Tell you what, you do your part to take care of this river, and I'll do mine. Okay?"

"It's a deal, Jewel. Maybe I'll even get Mrs. Gunderson and a few others to volunteer. Wouldn't that be something? Oh, and don't forget, Halloween is coming. Judging from some of the masks and clothes you folks were wearing tonight, you all would fit in real well. So keep that in mind. When it gets dark on the last day of October, lots of little masqueraders always come and stand outside my door and they yell at the top of their voices: 'Trick or treat! Smell my feet! Give me something good to eat!'"

"Well," Jewel says. "If we decide to dress up and stop by, you'll know it's us. We will have to yell something really different like: '*Trick or treat! We don't want no meat! Just give us black bananas to eat!*'"

"Sounds good to me," I joke. "I'll start buying lots of bananas and putting them aside, so they get nice and soft."

Jewel laughs and leans forward to kiss me on my cheek.

"Ah, at least that kiss was a tender one," I say. "Sure didn't want that vacuum cleaner coming at me again!"

We both laugh and hold hands for a few seconds.

"It's been quite a day, Raymondo. But you might want to keep most of what you've witnessed to yourself. Might be better that way."

"What if I decide to write a book about all of this?" I tease.

"Raymondo, if you did that, you'd have to label it fiction or fantasy. No one would believe you."

"Yeah," I answer. "Me? Write a book? That'll be the day."

I head up the hill, and for some reason I don't look back. But I do look up at that big moon and the stars. Tonight the sky is filled with thousands of stars, maybe even millions. There are definitely more than I have ever seen before. And to think they've been there all along.

Well, now I see them. And I think I know why.

EPILOGUE

A Not So Old Legend

There once were two brothers who lived in the same town, but they seldom saw each other. As the years went by, the distance between the two men grew greater and greater.

One day, the younger brother invited the older brother to go fishing. As boys, they sometimes fished along the Red River of the North. It was a river familiar to both men.

The two brothers met at a spot on the river where the catfish were said to be very large. As the men watched their bobbers, they began to reminisce. The men found it easier to talk when they faced the river instead of each other.

But that day, the bobbers weren't bobbing and the fish weren't biting. So the two men pulled in their lines and decided to do some exploring along the Red River—like they did when they were boys.

Within only a few minutes, the older brother found an old coin. He held it high and he became very excited.

"This coin was heads-up," the older brother shouted. "So it might be lucky as well as valuable."

As the younger brother searched, he did not find anything of interest for a rather long time. He was almost ready to give up and discontinue his search. But then he noticed a large pointed stone that was sticking out of the ground.

The younger brother called out to his older brother to come and take a look. Both men soon fell on their knees and began digging with their hands. They did this for hours.

Eventually, the men uncovered a huge stone that was shaped like a blacksmith's anvil. There were strange and intricate designs chiseled into all four sides of the stone. Yet, there was no way to lift the object out of the ground, for it weighed many hundreds of pounds.

By now, it was getting dark. The brothers decided to go home and meet at the same spot early the next morning.

When the two men returned to the site of the discovery, they saw the large hole that they had dug the previous day. But the great stone anvil was nowhere to be seen.

The men sat down beside the empty hole and were silent for a long time. Then the older brother spoke.

"Your discovery was the find of a lifetime," the older brother admitted. "And what a thrill to uncover it with nothing but our bare hands—just you and me! This, this is the stuff memories are made of."

After that day, the two brothers forged a new bond. Eventually, they were able to face each other again and express what was truly in their hearts.

Sometimes, when two individuals find something together, they become very close. And sometimes, when two individuals lose something together, they become even closer.

So say many of the "Unseen Ones" in the Red River Valley. And so says Jewel Rhee, the Sovereign of all the *Swanshees*. . . .

NOTES
&
ACKNOWLEDGMENTS

Strange as it may seem, *One Day on the River Red* was inspired by some unforgettable family stories that I heard when I was a boy growing up in Colorado. The stories dealt with my Aunt Margaret Sewald, to whom this book is dedicated. She died in the summer of 1938 and her sudden passing deeply affected our large extended family. Yet most of my cousins and I never knew her, though it seemed like we did. She haunted our homes, farms, and even the outlying fields for many years. Such is the power of stories.

A few weeks after Margaret's death, my father was irrigating sugar beets in a large field near Sterling, Colorado. It was a warm, moonlit night and there was a slight breeze. (Ditch water only was available when it was a family's "run," and that meant the family members sometimes had to irrigate both day and night until their assigned "run" was up.) In the semidarkness, my dad was convinced he saw the deceased Margaret standing in the middle of the beet field. Her hair was loose and hanging down, and it looked like she was beckoning to him. My father was not overly superstitious, but he broke out in a cold sweat. Maybe Margaret was letting him know that he was the next to leave this world?

Dad somehow summoned up the courage to actually approach the figure and see what the ghost of Margaret wanted. Maybe she was in need of Masses or novenas or prayers. When dad drew closer to the figure, he saw that it was not Margaret's ghost after all. It was a tall sunflower with a large head and big, broad leaves that were swaying in the wind. With his irrigation shovel, dad cut down the sunflower and breathed a sigh of relief. But the more he thought about it, the more he thought it might be some kind of sign. So right there in the middle of the beet field, he said a special prayer for the repose of his late sister-in-law's soul. On countless occasions, my father told that story, especially when we were irrigating at night. It was but one of many "Aunt Margaret stories."

In the 1920s and 1930s, the majority of my relatives worked in the sugar beet fields of northeastern Colorado. At that time, all of the thinning, hoeing, and harvesting had to be done by hand. Those who worked in the beet fields were called "stoop laborers." Bad as that sounds, it was far better than the frequently-heard phrase "dirty Rooshun beet workers."

Long before large numbers of Mexican-Americans arrived on the scene, German-Russian immigrants and their children did the backbreaking work in the beet fields. Like later immigrants, the Germans from Russia had to deal with long hours, low wages, inadequate housing, poor health care, discrimination, and even segregation. In many parts of Colorado, German-Russian districts and ethnic neighborhoods came into being: "Russia Town," "Little Moscow," "Little Saratov," "St. Petersburg," "The Jungles," and "The Rooshun Corner."

Like the rest of our relatives, Aunt Margaret and her brothers and sisters worked beets every spring, summer, and fall in Colorado. Their family was a large one (twelve children) and that meant they could complete a lot of acreage in a relatively short amount of time—if everyone worked, including the smallest children. But Margaret and her family were somewhat unusual in that they knew how to turn the drudgery of beet work into something of a grand adventure. One spring, they loaded up their old jalopy and drove hundreds of miles north to the Red River Valley of Minnesota and North Dakota. There they found ample work in the beet fields. A new sugar-processing facility was established in 1926 in East Grand Forks, Minnesota. Eventually, Margaret's parents rented a beet farm of their own southeast of the new sugar factory. But they and their children continued to work beets for other farmers to supplement the family's income.

When they would return to Colorado for visits, Margaret and

her other family members were more than eager to tell of their "North Country" experiences. They spoke of fertile soil that was almost as black as coal. And they pointed out that there was so much daylight up north, a family could work beets for fifteen to seventeen hours a day! The family members described how the nighttime sky sometimes would glow and shimmer with huge displays of the northern lights. "It was better than a picture show," they claimed. And they talked about the Red River, a narrow and heavily wooded river that flowed *north* into Canada.

The one "Aunt Margaret story" that really got my attention was how, one hot Sunday afternoon in Polk County, Minnesota, young Margaret (then only fourteen or so) and her girlfriend Peggy snuck off to have some fun. The girls waded into the murky waters of the Red River of the North. But Peggy evidently was too ashamed to admit she did not know how to swim. So she chose to wade into the water a short distance downstream from Margaret.

Before she knew it, Margaret's friend Peggy was in over her head and she found herself flailing around on the bottom of the Red River. But then something very unusual happened. As Peggy struggled and took in more and more water, a woman suddenly appeared and came to the young Peggy's aid. The woman had long hair and was dressed completely in white. She took hold of Peggy and helped her to shore. Then the mysterious woman disappeared.

Afterwards, when Margaret and Peggy dried off and hurried home, neither girl breathed a word about the near-drowning incident to their parents or family members. Otherwise, they knew they would never get permission to go anywhere or do anything on their own ever again.

Years later, when Margaret was living back in her home state of Colorado, she told the story of Peggy's near-drowning and the mysterious woman to someone she trusted—my mother. They were about the same age and they shared many stories about their personal experiences. But who, my mother asked Margaret, was the mysterious woman in the river? Was she an angel? A dead relative who decided to come to a loved one's aid? Or maybe a benevolent water spirit of some kind? Even Margaret was not quite sure.

The Germans from Russia had many beliefs relating to water and especially "*die Wassergeister*—the spirits of the water." In the irrigation country of Colorado, small children were warned never to get too close to any ditches that ran full of water. Otherwise, a *"Wasser Mann"* or a *"Wasser Frau"* might snatch and claim the little ones. Among the Catholic Volga Germans, there were even certain times of the year people had to be extremely careful around water. On Trinity Sunday (the first Sunday after Pentecost), swimming in a river or any body of water was strictly forbidden. It was believed that drownings and other mishaps would occur if people disturbed the "spirits of the water" on Trinity Sunday. (This belief was so strong that when Catholic Volga Germans emigrated from Russia to America, many took pains to avoid being at sea during the taboo time around Trinity Sunday.) As Catholic Volga Germans, Margaret and her family members were very much aware of these traditional beliefs.

When my mother first heard the story from Margaret about the near-drowning of "Peggy" on the Red River, Mom suspected the incident actually had happened to Margaret herself. "Peggy," after all, was a common nickname for girls named "Margaret." My mother noticed how emotional Margaret would get when she told that particular story. But my mother never asked Margaret directly about it. Mom knew that when young people told stories about "a friend," they sometimes were playing it safe and talking about themselves.

One reason my mother and Margaret were so close is that they lived together for several years. When my mother was still single, Margaret and her husband Jake (my mother's brother) moved in with my mom's parents. This was a custom from the Old

Country—when sons brought their wives to live in the home of the groom's parents. The institution of the "*Grossfamilie*" was not always an ideal arrangement, but it was sanctioned by generations of tradition. Everyone shared their wages, ate at the same table, and they took turns bathing in the same washtub. When Margaret and Jake had two daughters, my mother was the built-in babysitter who often watched the kids.

In 1934, my mother married and moved in with my father and his parents. But Mom remained in close contact with her favorite sister-in-law Margaret and managed to see her often. In early 1938, Margaret developed a goiter problem and that summer went into the local hospital for surgery. My mother went to the hospital to see Margaret and she seemed to be doing fine. "She was sitting up in bed and talking and then the next moment she fell over and was dead," my mother remembered. The doctors suspected the cause was a blood clot following surgery—perhaps a pulmonary embolism.

Margaret's sudden death in the summer of 1938 sent shockwaves through the German-Russian community in which she lived. "Although she died at twenty-six," my mother remembered many years later, "Margaret lived a full life. Unlike most of us, she traveled and she experienced a lot. Margaret was a bit of a rebel, but she was such fun to be around. There was never a dull moment with Margaret. I can still hear her laughter. And I think of her all the time."

My mother also recalled that Margaret was one of the first German-Russians in our community to be entrusted to a mortician for "preparation." Prior to that time, the German-Russians dressed and laid out the deceased in the largest room of the family home. An emotional three-day wake ensued, one filled with prayers, rosaries, holy water, incense, storytelling, and socializing. When the undertaker brought Margaret's embalmed body into my grandparents' home for the first day of the traditional wake, the mourners were horrified. The mortician had put a considerable amount of makeup on Margaret's face and he even painted her fingernails a bright red color. (In the 1920s and 1930s, conservative German-Russians considered extensive makeup and colorful nail polish to be "*egglich*" [ugly] and too "*weltlich*" [worldly].)

The sad task now fell upon my mother and her younger sister and their aged mother to sit beside Margaret's coffin and remove some of the makeup. They also had to file off the red fingernail polish. All three women wept as they worked. As my mother held her best friend's cold hands in her own, she cried especially hard. The death of Margaret was doubly difficult because she was several months pregnant with her third child when she died. "Poor Margaret," my mother later recalled. "Nothing about that day was easy—for her or for us. We felt like we were drowning in sorrow."

Where, my mother must have wondered during that incredibly dismal time, was the mysterious helper in Margaret's "river story"—the woman dressed completely in white? Did she come but once in a person's lifetime? Did she choose to rescue people only when they were drowning in deep water? Might the woman's identity finally be revealed to Margaret when she "crossed over to the other side"?

Memorable and powerful as the stories about my Aunt Margaret were, the stories were seldom consistent. As a child who never actually knew her, I was fascinated by how the "Aunt Margaret stories" would change somewhat depending on who the teller was. The women had their versions, the men had theirs, and the younger folks spun somewhat different tales. Such early exposure to multi-vocal storytelling undoubtedly influenced my decision to study Anthropology and Folklore when I went to college. In fact, I later earned a PhD in Folklore Studies from Indiana University in 1986. And I would teach folklore classes for more than three decades at North Dakota State University in Fargo.

During my years in both the classroom and the field, I often heard people relate family stories about near-drownings and mysterious helpers. For example, Troyd A. Geist and I included one such account in our volume, *Sundogs and Sunflowers: Folklore and Folk Art of the Northern Great Plains* (2010):

> *When I was little, my family and my aunts, uncles, and cousins were on a picnic on a sandbar in the Missouri River. The other kids and I were playing in the water. Our parents had marked off an area where we were supposed to play in to be safe. I got too far over on one side and was running through the water when I hit a drop-off.*
>
> *I remember that I wasn't scared because I could see this woman standing on the other side of me. She just stood there and watched me. My aunt and cousin were the first ones to get to me and pull me out.*
>
> *When I looked again, the lady was gone. When I told my mom what I had seen, she told me it must have been my guardian angel. I think maybe she was.*

The above story was told by a twenty-year-old student in the fall of 1987. She was from Bismarck, North Dakota—a city that lies right on the Missouri River. Her account is surprisingly similar to other stories about mysterious "river helpers," who suddenly appear and come to the aid of individuals who are drowning. When such stories are told in group settings, listeners often will nod their heads in an understanding fashion or offer similar accounts of their own.

Sometimes, truth is indeed "stranger than fiction." In December 1987, eleven-year-old Alvaro Garza, Jr., fell through the ice on the Red River near Fargo. By the time rescuers were able to come to his aid and pull the boy out of the river, Alvaro had been under the freezing waters for forty-five minutes. When the rescuers rushed him to the hospital, Alvaro's body temperature had fallen to only seventy-seven degrees. Yet Alvaro Garza, Jr., somehow survived.

Newspapers around the country carried articles about the incident and Alvaro was referred to as a "Christmas miracle." Since it was December, there was frequent talk of angels, spiritual helpers, and divine intervention. Alvaro grew to maturity, married, and had several children of his own. In 2001, his namesake, ten-year-old Alvaro Garza III, nearly drowned in a river in Texas. But he also was rescued and survived! The Garza family now has more than its fair share of "near-drowning" and "close call" stories. And the stories, while hair-raising and seemingly unbelievable, are instructive to other families who venture out on rivers at various times of the year.

My own family story about a near-drowning and a supernatural helper clearly does not stand alone. It has its parallel in other families, places, and traditional cultures. Such narratives provide intriguing evidence that when it comes to folklore and the art of storytelling, individuals of quite different backgrounds actually share much in common.

Many people had helped or inspired me by the time I wrote this novella in early 2018. In terms of the Scandinavian background, I am grateful to Alice Anderson and "The Sarah Circle" quilters, George Anderson, Sally Backman, Francie M. Berg, Rolf Berg, Pieper Bloomquist, Robin Carlson, Jeanine Ehnert, Paul T. Emch, Magnus Olafson, Marge Peterson, Sig Peterson, Sue Rusch, Rev. William C. Sherman, Audrey "The Lefse Lady" Smith, Dr. Playford Thorson, and the incomparable Norwegian-American performer and storyteller Judith Simundson.

For assistance with the German-Russian, Native American, and western North Dakota background, I am indebted to: Marianne Baron, Keith Bear, Elaine Brave Bull McLaughlin, Mary Louise Defender Wilson, Agatha Fool Bear, Julia Geiss, Rose Haman,

ONE DAY ON THE RIVER RED

Eddie "King" Johnson, Lynda Rose Johnson, Wade Keeps Eagle, Erwin Keller, Herman J. Kraft, Chris Leingang, Dr. Bea Medicine, Jim Nelson, Kathy Nelson, Sandra Poitra, Dr. A. C. Ross, Angeline Schneider, Flora Weinhandl, and the indomitable folk artist and raconteur Louis ("Mazakaga") Snider.

I also want to thank four of my esteemed colleagues for reading and reviewing my book when it was still a "work in progress." Their comments, insights, and suggestions proved very valuable and helpful: Tony Bender, Troyd A. Geist, Dr. Vernon Keel, and Dr. H. Elaine Lindgren. In addition, I thank Michael J. Kloberdanz, who edited my manuscript and did so more than once. On each occasion, he offered forthright and constructive criticism.

Suicide is a subject that I deal with in this novella. Although I use humor when writing about Raymond's suicide attempt, I do not consider suicide itself a laughing matter. I am one of the many, many people who has struggled "to make some sense of it all" in the aftermath of a loved one's suicide. Anyone dealing with suicidal thoughts or emotional distress should contact the National Suicide Prevention Lifeline (1-800-273-8255). There is someone available at that number around the clock. The staff members at the NSPL offer expert assistance and they literally help save lives every single day.

Last but certainly not least, I want to thank the members of my immediate family for their constant encouragement, support, and unconditional love: Rosalinda ("Rosi"), Mike, Paula, Matt, and little Danci. Every moment that I have spent with each of them on the Red River of the North has been a "jewel." And as a result, I feel truly blessed. As little Elisa in my story so lovingly says: "*Merci mille fois plus*—Thank you a thousand times and more."

About the Author

Timothy J. Kloberdanz has lived in the Red River Valley of North Dakota for more than forty years. He has traveled the entire length of the Red River of the North—from Wahpeton, North Dakota, and Breckenridge, Minnesota, to Lake Winnipeg in Manitoba, Canada.

The author earned academic degrees at the University of Colorado (Boulder), Colorado State University (Fort Collins), and Indiana University (Bloomington). "Yet my real education," he admits, "took place not in classrooms but in my one-on-one interactions with elders of different backgrounds. Several of them lacked any kind of formal schooling. Nonetheless, they could see to the heart of things. And they helped open my eyes to an incredibly wide range of possibilities and wonders."

Although he is "retired," Dr. Kloberdanz continues to do ethnographic and literary research in the Great Plains region and in other parts of the American West. A professor emeritus at North Dakota State University, he taught more than eight thousand students and received many awards during his academic career. He is the author or co-author of several books and has written numerous articles and other pieces, including a script for a prize-winning public television documentary.

Along with his wife Rosalinda, Dr. Kloberdanz currently makes his home in Fargo, North Dakota. "Fargo is renowned for its wicked winds and bone-numbing winters," the author writes. "But these realities are balanced by occasional gentle breezes and brilliant displays of the great northern lights."

One Day on the River Red is Timothy J. Kloberdanz's first novella.

www.ingramcontent.com/pod-product-compliance
Lightning Source LLC
Chambersburg PA
CBHW050800250626
47155CB00005B/2146